FISH ANTHOLOGY

2005

The Mountains of Mars

and Other Stories

www.fishpublishing.com

FISH ANTHOLOGY
2005

Winners of the 2004/5
Fish Short Story Prize

Edited by Clem Cairns

Assistant Editors
Lorraine Bacchus
Tessa Gibson
Jula Walton

Fish Publishing

Durrus, Bantry, Co. Cork, Ireland

www.fishpublishing.com

This book is dedicated to

the readers who have short listed stories for the

Fish Anthologies over the last eleven years.

Published in Ireland by
Fish Publishing, 2005
Durrus, Bantry, Co. Cork

This book is published with the assistance of The Arts Council of Ireland.

The Short Story Prize is run with assistance from Anam Cara Writers' and Artists' Retreat. www.anamcararetreat.com

ISBN 0-9542586-3-0

A catalogue record of this book is available from the British Library.

Cover painting, *All That Remains,* by Dearbhail Connon
Cover design by Jula Walton

For details on Fish Publishing's Annual Short Story Prize see back of book.
Or write to:

Fish Short Story Prize, Durrus, Bantry, Co. Cork, Ireland
info@fishpublishing.com

Or see our website - www.fishpublishing.com

What is Fish Publishing?

The Fish Short Story Prize is an open door that's inviting writers to walk through it. It has to be encouraged, celebrated, congratulated.
Roddy Doyle

Fish is doing great work. It's an inspiration for all new writers.
Frank McCourt

Fish is an independent outfit dedicated to fostering and publishing new talent. Since the first Fish Short Story Prize in 1994 we have published over 150 writers, many of whom have subsequently developed successful writing careers.

Most of the stories we receive come from English-speaking countries, but we welcome stories from all over the world. So far we have published writers from Indonesia, Nepal, Singapore, The Middle East and Africa. We would love to publish more from these and other places.

In 2004 we added the One Page Story Prize and the Unpublished Novel Award, and we are currently running a Short Histories Prize for the British Historical Novel Society. We have also developed and expanded the Critique Service to include the Fish Editorial Consultancy for writers who require a longer-term in-depth assessment of their work. Some information on all of these can be found at the back of this book, or in full at www.fishpublishing.com

Forthcoming Events

The Short Histories Prize closes on 30 August 2005. The anthology of winning stories will be in the shops in 2006.

The Fish Short Story Prize closes on 30 November 2005, and the One Page Prize on 4 March 2006. The resulting Anthology will be launched at the West Cork Literary Festival during the last week of June 2006.

Nick Wright won the Inaugural Unpublished Novel Award with *The Language Me Feel It*, and we expect to publish it later this year.

Contents

Foreword

Waiting for the final selection of 15 stories to come back from the judges is always a thrill. But this year, with an exceptionally busy schedule, I had had no sneak preview of the short-listed stories, and I couldn't wait to see what the 2005 Anthology had in store.

Well ... I'm delighted.

The winning story, 'Mountains of Mars', by Marc Phillips makes a great title to the Anthology, and the story, full of understated tension, kicks the book off wonderfully. Enjoy your €10,000 first prize, Marc. Second, Jo Campbell's story, 'In the Desert', is surely a woman's story, of loss late in life and the possibility of redemption. I'll be re-reading this one in my middle-age. Second prize of a week at the Anam Cara Writers' and Artists' Retreat in the stunning location of the Beara Peninsula goes to Jo. Sue Booth-Forbes' hospitality and the special ambience at the retreat is a recipe for a productive week. Thanks to Sue for donating this generous prize.

I'm pleased that the judges selected two of Barry Troy's stories - 'A Life', insightfully written, about a teenage girl whose mother has left her to cope with a drunken father and a house-full of kids, and in third place, 'Booker Night in Baggot Street' - hilarious - a most unlikely discussion develops in a Dublin pub while watching the Booker Prize on TV. It would make a great play.

It's refreshing to have so many humorous stories in the Anthology. It's difficult to write successful comedy but Tomás O'Beirne succeeds in his eccentric story 'The Missing Taxi Man'. So too does Caroline Koeppel in her story, 'How to Kill a Latin Teacher', which left me with the eerie feeling that I may have missed an opportunity with my own Latin teacher! Selma Dabbagh's story, 'Beirut-Paris-Beirut', was simply masterful. And Mary Leland's 'Skin Song', a sensual tale told from the point of view of Geraldine, a young girl observing her mother's intimate relationship with the music teacher, and her own parallel coming of age, is erotically atmospheric, beautifully paced and unfolds with a timeless quality that had me totally absorbed.

A special thank you to the three judges, Frank Delaney, Julia Neuberger and Morgan Llywelyn, who put a huge amount of time and consideration into their selection of the 15 short stories that are published in this anthology. The short list comprised ninety stories, whittled from a long list of 200 by our editorial panel. I know how much care is taken over this, and how difficult it is to turn so much fantastic work away. Let's hope those writers who didn't make the cut do the necessary tweaks and enter again next year. In total there were 1,800 stories entered into the 2004/5 Fish Short Story Prize. Thank you all for sending your work - so much artistic endeavour - it's wonderful. We at Fish get much pleasure reading your stories, and it reaffirms that we're doing the right thing.

The One Page Story Prize has been inspirational. I absolutely love all the ones in this book. Which one stands out for me - they all do! But Rob Pateman's 'God's Fingerprint', Richard Dunford's 'A Typical Wednesday' and Paul Bassett Davies' 'Imaginary Friend' are getting a special mention for their sheer brilliance and for giving me a different perspective. This year's judge, Dave Eggers, had much trouble picking 10 from the short list of 40, and then had the bright idea of sharing the glory of winning the competition (and the prize money of €1,000), between his two favourites - 'Postcard From New York' by Tom Murray and 'Believe It' by Brian Tiernan. In less than 251 words all of these authors have managed to conjure up personalities, scenes and a story to go with them. The qualities of the poet are needed to write so succinctly.

I would love to be able to publish more of the 1,700 entered. Maybe Fish should have a book for one page stories alone. They certainly are worthy.

Jula Walton
May 2005

Acknowledgements

Frank Delaney, Julia Neuberger and Morgan Llywelyn for judging the Fish Short Story Prize, and Dave Eggers for judging the One Page Story Prize.

Clem Cairns for keeping the whole show on the road.

The editorial staff – Carmel Winters, Yann Kelly Hoffman, Claire Kelly Hoffman, Emily Murison, Lorraine Bacchus, Naomi Brandel, Karen Kenny, Daithi Muldoon, Francis Humphrys, Maggie Sweeney, Maureen O'Sullivan, Tessa Gibson, Eithne Ní Mhurchu, Geralyn McCarthy, Julia Fairlie, Valerie Gould, Katie Gould, Penny Gray, Mary Hawkes, Tadgh Fallon, Jennifer Spohn, Viv Jenkins, Ailish Butler, Lothar Luken and Rachel Bell.

Jula Walton for book and cover design, Jock Howson for his elegant solutions, executive lunches and co-ordinating web matters. Lorraine Bacchus and Tessa Gibson for administration. Trevor Williams of Traintrain New Media and Phoebe Bright of Vivid Logic for their web work. Dearbhail Connon for the cover image and John O'Sullivan and Mary Ross in An Post.

The Mountains of Mars

Marc Phillips

The phone rings again. He hears it. She kicks him.

"Don't kick me."

"The phone's ringing."

"I hear it."

"Well get it."

"Hello." The bed creaks. "No. You got the wrong number."

"Was that Darryl?"

"You heard me say wrong number."

Darryl doesn't call any more, doesn't come over any more either. She knows that. Darryl is a drinker in the occupational sense, like he, himself, was. Since Thanksgiving, their ninth anniversary, her man had not had a drink. He didn't say anything about it, just stopped. Now Darryl doesn't know him down at the Shell station and won't recognize him at Stockman's Feed. She looks over his chest at the clock.

"It's three o'clock. Who calls at three o'clock?"

"Yeah. I didn't ask," he says, "I was about to get up at four anyway. Can you make us some eggs?"

"Might as well."

He heads for the shower and she rises to light up the kitchen. She passes Big Boy on the couch and thinks she'll let her husband wake him up. Rousting the young man is like rolling a boulder out of a steep mud hole.

He doesn't use soap this morning – a thing left over from his hunting days. Only scalding hot water and her sea sponge. He doesn't hunt any more because he kills more deer than he'd rather protecting their apple trees. They give away cuts of venison as it is. And he never found the beneficial trade-off in cleaning small game. He doesn't use deodorant either. These are hard habits to break when heading to the woods. He comes out in Carhartt and insulated Hi-Lo country earth tones and he looks like he should have a gun. He'll think about it over his eggs and toast and he'll pack a pistol before they leave. This is natural, like packing a canteen.

The coffee is so strong he can tell she did it for his sake. It's nearly pudding. There's half a fifth of Jack Daniels near the coffee maker, beside the creamer. Neither of them takes sugar. There's no bowl out for that. The black labeled bottle with its liquid oaken charcoal catches the sun, late mornings, and makes for good counter art. Big Boy liked to have some from time to time, with fresh mint from the yard, or without. Somebody will drink it.

She says, "Can I ask you a question? You didn't stop drinking for health reasons, did you?"

"Partly."

"Were you hurting anywhere?" She puts cheese in the eggs.

"There's some things I've got to get done, is all. It's easier this way."

"They're almost ready. You better wake him up." He starts to go in there. She says, "Hey. You're the strongest man I've ever known. Inside and out."

"Thanks, honey."

"Where will you go?" She doesn't wonder *why* they go.

"The base of the Capitans, West Mountain, I think."

They will go not because camping those mountains is a better recreation than anything else (though it is, out here), but because those mountains feel like the rising reason for everything else. To some. And they merit visiting.

"Watch after him?" she asks; her sister's oldest child.

"Yes."

~

Big Boy ties the canvas off on the Jeep's rack and stretches it taut with galvanized poles and guylines over the flat spot closest to the little pond. They are sixteen miles north of Highway 380. Ten of those are rutted, rocky, pitted miles that a vehicle has got to be designed to withstand more than once.

West Mountain sits guard over the water hole like an enormous child with a puddle of prized marbles between his legs. 8,011 feet of it rise to the north and long foothills stretch out along the east and west borders of the clearing. Great blue spruce and fir trees keep the dawning and setting sun off the water for another hour on each side. It is the only year-round standing water in a million acres this side of the Valley of Fire. To the south they can see the lip of the endless dry bowl called the Tularosa Basin. It looks like it would hold the Pacific Ocean.

Nobody litters here. The only evidence of man other than the worn trail is a metallic yellow sign riveted to a chunk of gray stone resembling an Angus steer with his head bent to the weeds. By the time a visitor sees the pond from the trail, he sees the sign. "Operation Game Thief $750 Reward." The rest of it is printed small enough that a man has to be interested in what it says to read.

Big Boy's supposed to dig a fire ring and look for suitable rocks.

His uncle had suggested he pull on that whiskey. Get him going. He digs a good pit and has it lined with stones, one tall and flat one in the middle to fit a Dutch oven. He's making a pine bough bed when his uncle drags down two small aspen trees, one at a time, from where last year's snow snapped them forty feet up the mountain's face. Big Boy takes a deep pull on the whiskey bottle and offers it to his uncle.

"Thanks. I gave it up."

"Oh," he says. He screws the top on the bottle and searches for a place to put it away. He looks like he's fired off a cussword in Sunday school.

"It's alright. I wouldn't have let you bring it if it bothered me."

"I don't want to drink if you're not."

"You can drink like you do for the rest of your life. Live to a hundred. You'll still die way short of the booze I've had. Drink up. I really don't care."

Big Boy sticks the bottle in his bed roll.

"Tell me if I'm boring sober."

Big Boy says he will. They whittle on the trees for kindling and build a nice teepee of wood shavings in the fire ring. The wood is damp. It's a matter of pride in the things his uncle wants to be sure Big Boy knows – in addition to what he picks up at college – that they do not use paper or gasoline or anything but a fistful of sedge and a match to light the fire.

"I've got a laundry list of things built up inside me that I need to deal with. You understand? But not out here. You stop me. I don't want to be an ass about it."

Big Boy doesn't understand that. He tells his uncle it looks like snow. The man says the gap develops its own weather, in a way it sees fit. Snow is fine. Bring it.

They organize the camp and take off on a short hike around mid-afternoon. The man has his Ruger .44 on his hip. On the other side of a granite outcropping, about a mile from camp, they walk up on a bull elk standing in a clearing. It stands as tall as a quarter horse and has a rack as wide as the Jeep's bumper. Ten seconds more and his cow steps out behind him. She's smaller, but still over five hundred pounds of graceful beast. The four of them stand and look at one another for a long time. Then the cow walks out the other side of the clearing. The bull keeps an eye on these two guys until she's gone, and he goes too. That's the first and second elk Big Boy's ever seen in person and the first ones his uncle could ever throw a stick and hit, though he's been coming to these mountains for many years now. The short hike turns long and neither of them minds so much.

~

They tire of jokes and run low on conversation not long after dark. The afternoon's hike has both of them wanting to rest. They take to their beds – wool blankets draped over fragrant, springy pine – and each comments on what a comfortable job they've made of them. Big Boy tips the whiskey back twice to take the rattle from his teeth since he shed his coat. Sleep comes fast and deep.

It's ten past ten when the four-wheelers pass their camp on the way up. The rumble wakes the man and he looks at the glowing green hands of his Casio. Big Boy is watching the headlamps dart from tree to tree as well, never falling directly on the Jeep.

"What the hell," Big Boy says.

"No telling."

An hour later, the pounding crack of a large-bore rifle removes any question. Their camp is inside the echo, so the shot came from somewhere nearby on the other side of the pond. Within a quarter mile. Neither of them is asleep. In another thirty minutes, the engines start again and the light beams skitter closer from the other way.

Alert and wary now, they count the vehicles as they approach. Big Boy on his belly, and his uncle propped on one elbow. Five. Moonlight and reflected headlights give them a good silhouette of the riders. He doesn't say it to Big Boy, but the man's glad their fire has no visible embers, glad they took the Jeep so close to the water, even though the ground was a little damp.

Then he looks closely at the lead rider, a rifle across the front rack, nothing on the rear. Number two, nothing bulging behind him. Number three has two riders, nothing back there. Number four is a kid, no rack at all. He opens his eyelids wide and fixes on the last one. Finally the thing clears the moonshade of evergreens and throws an outline on the screen of blue stars. A rider and a rifle is all. Damn it.

He thinks he hears the engines for a solid two minutes. That places their camp over a mile away, far enough not to spook the game drinking here at night. They must've arrived when he and Big Boy were hiking. Neither of them heard the party setting up camp.

"They'll be back at first light."

"You think so?" Big Boy asks.

"Trust me. If they missed, they'd still be up there."

"So they killed something?"

"An elk I'm guessing. Something too big for those four-wheelers. It's gutted and hanging in a tree somewhere. Keep the mountain lions off it."

Big Boy sees his uncle's head turn this way and that, considering. He asks, "What do you want to do?"

"We can't stay here." The Casio says 12:05.

"Go home?"

"I don't want to pass their camp on the way down. Maybe drive on to the summit for tonight. Come back after they've cut that thing up and gone." The Casio says 12:06. "I hate to drive that trail at night, though. Steep and real narrow."

"So. What do you think?"

"Pack it up and we'll see."

~

He tells his nephew Forestry can take that reward money and hire another game warden. It aint enough for him to cross five armed men.

"Six. One four-wheeler had two on it."

"One of them was a kid."

"Oh." Big Boy hadn't noticed that. "Still be a nice chunk of change."

They are in the middle of the trail, two thousand feet above the pond, well past where the four-wheeler tracks veered off. The trail's not wide enough to have more than a middle in this spot, and the drop-off on the driver's side is nearly parallel with the few tree trunks that dot it. The Jeep is crammed with their gear – the best they could do without turning on a lantern – and facing downhill, ready to get back to their spot when the poachers are gone. The summit is too far, too cold, and too dangerous at night. Not where they want to spend the next four nights anyway. Instead, they would sleep in the Jeep seats and pitch camp by the water again in the morning and nap half the day.

They don't sleep. Big Boy talks about some of his freshman classes, a new friend he's made named Scott, and rehashes his decision against playing college football. His uncle silently and brutally thrashes himself for getting run off like that. He could be in a minivan with a fat wife and two fat kids and a yappy rat-dog, saying how gosh darn lucky they were and there are dangerous people in the world.

They didn't see any hanging carcass from the trail on their slow climb. But they weren't really looking. The man would wager his nephew a hundred dollars he could find the thing with a quickness, in pitch dark. He mulls over the $750 question and thinks about saying to Big Boy that it's not their job to patrol the forest. Somebody else's job. But his nephew knows at least that much without being told, again.

He and Darryl would have done just this. They would have thrown their gear in the Jeep and scooted on up this trail. Then they would have tossed that bottle back and forth until most of it was gone and eased back down to the poached elk on foot. Hidden in two separate spots within sight of it, they would've gotten the drop on those ole boys. They would've taken somebody's driver's license to serve irrefutably as "information leading to a conviction." $375 apiece. They'd have gone down to the track in Ruidoso Downs the next day and wouldn't have remembered the drive home.

A new sun lights on shame first of all, then exposes regret and indecision. It's a hard dawn to tolerate.

~

Twenty-seven hours and five minutes it had taken Big Boy to get back to the house. A full minute before he can make coherent words, his aunt stares wide-eyed and agape at him. She waits. He tells. The shot in the night, the four-wheelers, the Jeep is trash, her husband's on foot. The Ford. He does not say that something in his gut feels busted or the ankle inside one of his boots is swelled so grotesquely that the leather will have to be cut away. It's finally numb from the constriction, and this is the only reason he's able to walk on it. She says his lip is flayed and one of his front teeth is broken in half. He says it doesn't hurt even a little bit. She's got to call the law and he's taking his own truck back up there. Where are his uncle's guns?

No, he is *not* going back up there!

In the twenty-eighth hour, she slides Big Boy's truck to a sputtering stall in front of Capitan Village Hall beside the police truck. Big Boy climbs out of the passenger seat and doesn't quite beat her to the door. She ushers him inside and says tell it again. Coffee mugs sit untouched and eventually cease steaming. A ringing phone goes unanswered and the chief has his deputy get on the radio when Big Boy gets to the part about the rifle round going all the way through the Jeep, back to front, through their gear, and splashing up bits of the plastic dash.

"Son, we need to get you to the clinic across the street," the chief says.

"I'm ok. I'm going up there to find him."

"No. We're going home," his aunt says.

"You're not doing either," the chief tells them. "They'll go through that Jeep and figure out where you live soon enough." What he's thinking is after they shoot the man in his head, they'll try to head off Big Boy before he talks. "It's not safe. He goes to the doctor and you stay here."

"My husband's on his way home. I intend to be there." She pushes Big Boy out the door by his shoulder and toward the clinic over there. He turns and walks to the passenger door again and says he's really, really not hurt. He'll go home with her and wait. If that's all he can do.

She's got his boot cut off with pruning sheers and is busy cleaning his face. He's had some aspirins. The ice on his ankle is making it hurt so bad. He wants to vomit but he doesn't dare.

He says, "He won't come back here with them on his ass."

"Hard-headed. Hard-headed ..." She's crying when she cracks the kitchen window with the first aid kit. "Bastard!"

At the top of the thirty-first hour, a chopper pilot and a forest ranger stand over Big Boy's shoulder as he fingers a USDA topographic map on the pine plank table. Another man in a gusseted oilcloth barn coat and fatigue bottoms stands near the door with his watch cap in his hands.

"We camped here." "The shot came from over this way." "We drove up here for the night." "We came back down around eight. Passed them here." "The Jeep's wrapped around a tree up in here. No, here. I think."

"How many?"

"Five. And one kid." "Huh?" "I don't know." "A red pick-up. Ford, maybe."

"Where'd he go?"

"Don't know. He told me to climb and circle west. Go home." "He's got a forty-four." "I heard two shots. Didn't sound like a rifle."

By the fortieth hour, they've got them. Nobody can hide a truck from a helicopter in the high desert. The kid – a slight thirteen-year-old who lives right down West Lobo from them – breaks first and the others confess in succession. The chief's pinching his temples with a gloved hand on the side porch when she opens the door. His other hand is on the butt of his sidearm. He's so sorry. The poachers are pretty sure they hit her husband at least once before they lost his track. They haven't found him yet. She's not supposed to give up though. He shot at them with that pistol late last night. He got the truck. Probably her husband and nephew will get the Game Thief money, is what he's hearing. The talk, you know. Sorry.

"We've got eight horsemen, Lincoln County, Alto, Carrizozo, and Ruidoso deputies out there looking. Forestry is bringing in two dozen more and a busload of smoke jumpers. We'll find him." He leaves.

It's not good enough, and no longer a matter of safety to stay home. On Highway 380, on their way to the trailhead, she asks Big Boy the question.

"How many did he have?"

"Six. The box is still in the Jeep."

"Can I get your truck up there?"

"Probably not. He won't be up there anyway. If he's … If he –"

"Where would he be, Big Boy?"

"He sent me uphill. I think that was him I heard shooting. He would've run them the other way."

"Tell me."

"Head for the gap and take the last way to the right at the base of the hill."

She slaps the steering wheel. The bumps hurt Big Boy, every little one. The big ones are almost unbearable. He makes no sound and refuses to adjust himself in the seat, afraid she'll stop or take him back to the house.

It takes so long to cover the distance among the pits and washouts that it's driving them crazy. But if she goes any faster his little truck will rattle to scrap metal.

"He told me a week before you got here," she says. "He said he wanted to volunteer somewhere. Out of the blue. A hospital or something."

"We'll find him. He aint dead."

"Can you believe that? Him. Volunteer."

"He's just waiting, is all. He doesn't know they're caught."

"Never waited on a Goddamn thing. Not once. He'd of set the whole mountain on fire."

~

His brother flew into El Paso and drove a rental car up the same day the chopper pilot had taken his machine back to Santa Fe. He bought two cutting horses from the stable north of town, and saddles too.

It's hour seventy-three and Big Boy takes it in spurts and chews on pain pills and they ride the gap and the valley in crisscross patterns for every minute the sun shines. The official search party gives it up on the fourth day and they take their bullhorns and two hounds with them. The two men ride and holler their voices flat. They ride stubborn streaks out of the animals. They get off and walk them, snorting and sweating, down through arroyos and gingerly through cactus patches. Big Boy's ankle cast has dirt packed into the open toe. It doesn't fit in the stirrup. He has taken to reigning his mount round and round in a tight circle until he spots weeds standing up somewhere. He throws his heels into the flanks of the stout Quarter Horse and it squats and lunges and they take off in a galloping charge to that spot to look and they trample those weeds down.

"Presumed dead" spills out of the TV and radio on every frequency. "experienced outdoorsman ... on foot ... DEAD." "local man ... bizarre twist ... DEAD." "stalked ... shot ... DEAD." She listens to it all and doesn't eat much. Capitan Interdenominational had started the casserole parade and the town took the cue and followed suit. She's got food on top of food where she can't see the countertop and a freezer full of shit she doesn't want. She has to erase and reset the answering machine three times a day. It's not friends. They only have three. But it's relatives, the news, family of the poachers, and people she couldn't pick out of a crowd on a bet. Can she believe? – that people would go to such lengths to keep from getting arrested for poaching! Belief is not an issue with which she struggles. When she was talking still, she was telling them they needn't bother to sit with her. If they wanted to help, go look. His brother asked her to quit that because those people got in his way.

When the TV's off, the ceiling fan ticks like a metronome, setting time so slow that afternoons are inescapable expanses. So the box is on now. A big man who runs the water department had taken to stacking firewood on the porch like a benevolent phantom. She caught him once and he apologized if he scared her. Didn't want to bother her, but she has to stay warm. He's split these into fours, but he can try to get them into eighths if they're still a little heavy.

"They'll be fine."

Her brother-in-law opens the door at three o'clock. All the curtains are drawn and the afternoon light startles her like a trumpet blast. He doesn't speak soon enough to have good news or no news. She knows.

"I want to see him." She takes her purse from the coffee table.

"I don't think you do."

"I'll go by myself if you don't take me."

The police hadn't taken the body anywhere yet, so they ride together toward the trailhead down 380 in his rented Buick.

"I don't think this car will make it far on that trail," she says. "Will it?"

"He's in a culvert under the highway."

"Oh God," and she loses it before she can hide her face in her hands. She trembles.

He hopes she'll change her mind and they can turn around. The winter wind had kept the stink off his brother's body, but that was the only nastiness spared.

"Where's Big Boy?"

"Talking to him. He wouldn't leave. I want you to come back to North Carolina with me."

They'd already talked about this. She says no again, but doesn't thank him for the offer this time.

"At least go to your mama's."

Maybe she will.

She stands in the dry creek bed and stares into the massive concrete tube, a tunnel easily big enough for cattle to pass through, her husband in profile, a grotesque memorial to himself. He's leaning back on the concavity with his legs crossed Indian style and his chin is on his chest. She can see his left side and the big black pistol still in his left hand. She doesn't really see Big Boy sitting cross-legged facing the dead man until a Lincoln County sheriff's deputy walks past her and bends to take the young man by an arm to coax him out of there.

Big Boy pushes the deputy back by the belt buckle with one hand and doesn't look away from his uncle.

"Wait," she says. "I'll get him out." She barely has to stoop to walk into the culvert.

She puts a hand on Big Boy's shoulder. "Hey," she whispers. "We've got to go."

He crawls out on his hands and knees. Then she looks down on her husband and sees the ball of his right shoulder is gone. That side of his jacket and the chest of his shirt are black. His exposed skin has turned shark belly gray and unnatural wrinkles are frozen in place on his face and neck. The brightest thing in the picture is a round piece of bone laid bare just outside the collar of his jacket. Some reason the refracted afternoon light called on it to testify, she can't figure why.

The deputy says, "Ma'am?"

She turns to leave before anyone can put a hand on her, and she sees a large pockmark and a jagged crack in the concrete where Big Boy was sitting. She steps over to put her finger in it, then turns around and sees a similar mark on the concrete, inches above her husband's head. A mashed bullet lodged in it.

Coming out, the round opening frames for her the last view her man had. It's a cameo portrait of the ten thousand foot peaks, East and West Mountain, so far away they each look no bigger than the hill in their driveway. Between here and there is a distance not worth considering without a truck or a horse. Shot and run like an animal. His mountains with their hiding places could be anywhere. With their trees, anywhere at all.

"Where were they caught?" she asks the deputy, once out in the creek bed.

"Not anywhere near here. Way over that way." He points to the far base of West Mountain. "Like they thought he'd circled back or they gave up entirely. The holes in there are from his pistol. We think he died with the hammer back. When the rigor mortis set in, his fing-"

"That's not helpful," her brother-in-law tells the man.

"No. Of course not. I'm very sorry, ma'am."

"So he had a bullet left," she says.

"Two, I think. There's one still in there." the deputy responds.

"I wish they'd of stumbled onto him, then. Before he died."

His brother says, "Damn it." He says, "I do too."

"Me too," Big Boy whispers.

The deputy nods. "It wouldn't have been a bad thing."

In the Desert

Jo Campbell

Under my feet I feel the tiny, tiny, perpetual shifting of the sand. I brace my legs against it, and against the heat that is flowing through me, because when I move it must be deliberately. I am on the edge now; there is no room for mistakes.

Ten yards away, her back to me, Cassie is perching insecurely on her kneeling camel.

On our first night here I stood at the window in the dark and told myself *I am in Africa,* but I felt nothing. The marmoreal hotel, the antiseptic swimming-pool and the well-groomed palms might have been in Torquay. The cuisine at dinner had been Torquay with harrissa.

It's nice, isn't it? said Cassie. *Very comfortable. And so warm! In February!*

Her eyes pleaded with me

Fine, I said. *Really. It's fine.* I smiled at her. Tunisia had been her idea.

A death lays you open to the kindness of others. Sooner or later you have to respond to their loving concern for you to get up, get over it, get a grip, get a life. Your misery undermines their optimism, their faith that everything is in the end remediable. They cannot bear it, and if you persist in it they will abandon you altogether.

I came to Tunisia because I did not want Cassie to abandon me. Taking the holiday seemed a tolerable way to let her know that I appreciated what she was trying to do, that her efforts were not in vain. I did not have to enjoy myself as long as she believed I did.

And if that makes me sound a miserable bitch, well, that's something else Death does to you. Did to me.

In the mornings we swim from the hotel beach: Cassie prefers it to the pool. Afterwards the barman in the beach kiosk makes us cappuccinos decorated with hearts and flowers in chocolate. He has time for such flourishes; the hotel is half-empty and the rest of the clientele, retired people like ourselves, are not enthusiastic swimmers. Later we dress, and walk five hundred yards along the sea road to the dinky little modern marina, full of beautiful and expensive yachts, perpetually moored. We browse round the waterside boutiques and jewellery shops, and eat lunch in a timidly ethnic café, choosing with due regard to the limitations of ageing digestions and the risks of picking up salmonella. Time passes, quite pleasantly.

I find the evenings more difficult. Cassie is an attractive and gregarious woman; she likes people. She thinks I need company, particularly male company, and she has a mission to provide it; she is busy winnowing out the very few unattached men in the hotel. I have seen her do this before, in other contexts. She is animated, she is charming, she draws them in. Then, as the bar piano tinkles away or the ersatz belly-dancers perform their tired routines, I hear her make a tactful reference to her husband at home and add, lowering her voice, *poor Eunice lost her husband two years ago.* As if I had only to look properly to find Donald mislaid at the back of a cupboard or kicked out of sight beneath a bed.

The men usually take the disappointment on the chin and, after only a momentary pause, turn courteously to me. But I am awkward and unresponsive.

I have lost the automatic confidence I had as Donald's wife; I cannot place myself in these exchanges; I cannot pick up the proper tone. At sixty-one I am experiencing all the gaucherie of fifteen.

On the third morning of our stay, we take a taxi into Sousse: still tourist land, but livelier and less sterile than our concrete enclave. We visit the old town, eat a lunch full of spice and flavour, go shopping in the noise and heat of the casbah. Cassie's opulent figure and dark hair and eyes appeal strongly to the Tunisians. *You are Arabic woman,* cry the shopkeepers; *beautiful Arabic woman,* they croon, draping her with kaftans and scarves, holding up before her necklaces of lapis lazuli and bracelets of cornelian, while she fidgets and hangs on to her handbag and I droop in the doorway, my custom unsolicited, a neglected English rose.

In the afternoon we visit one of the sights of Sousse, a traditional Arab merchant's house of former days, tastefully restored. A serious young woman, her head covered, conducts us round the outer rooms, used for business, the cool interior courtyard with its little fountain, the separate quarters for the women and children, the special curtained bed, built into an alcove in the wall, in which man and wife could be together.

We women had our rights too, she says, blushing faintly.

She points out a candle in a sconce beside the bed.

When the husband had intercourse with his wife he was supposed to – continue whilst the candle burned, to make sure she was satisfied.

She beams, inviting us to admire this evidence of advanced thinking.

What if it didn't work? whispers Cassie.

She got a longer candle. Or something.

We snort with laughter down our noses, and the guide frowns at us; *I did not expect this,* her look says, *from mature ladies like you.*

Tonight Cassie parades the best of her finds; she has high hopes of this one. He is a quiet-spoken, open-faced man, a little rounded in outline, a little bald of pate. He talks to me about music; he is knowledgeable, and interesting. I allow myself to be interested. He lives in North London, as I do.

Perhaps we might go to a concert together sometime, he says.

That would be nice, I say, after a pause.

Not nice enough, he says lightly.

I'm sorry, I say.

No hard feelings. Here, take my phone number – you might change your mind.

Cassie is disappointed in me.

Why not? she says later. *Why not go to a concert with the man? He's nice enough, isn't he?*

Quite nice enough, I say. *It's me – I'm not ready for all that.*

All what? says Cassie, *It'd just be a concert.*

Other possibilities could arise, couldn't they? Even at my age.

Well of course, says Cassie, *and why not? If you liked each other? If you became friends? Don't you miss it?*

It's not the thing you miss, I say.

I'm lying, of course. It's not important, compared with the other things you miss – a voice, a laugh, an arm around you in the small hours – but you do miss it. Your body misses it, with a sort of sullen growling dissatisfaction, *I am not nourished, feed me now.* Your mind goes on permanent alert, so that a phrase read or overheard, an image glimpsed, can betray you into hectic longing or schoolgirl ribaldry. These are not overwhelming feelings, you remain in control, even grimly amused by them. They are not powerful enough to warrant the labour of cultivating a friendship, the anxious negotiations of ageing, unfamiliar bodies.

I couldn't face getting my kit off for someone new, I tell Cassie.

Now I need a sop to feed her, a token of enjoyment and interest.

Perhaps we should sign up for the Sahara expedition after all, I say.

This is a two-day coach tour, taking in visits to a famous casbah, an oasis, some spectacular Roman ruins. The high spot is a camel-ride into the desert, to see the sunset over the dunes. It is quite expensive, and consequently undersubscribed. We add our names to the list in the hotel atrium.

I don't know about this camel-ride, says Cassie on the coach.

We have already travelled a long way. Through the coach window we have seen a series of pictures; mosques, minarets, villages; a goatherd, clad head to ankle in a dark burnous, outlined against the morning sky. From time to time we have been given brief opportunities to step into the picture. We have wandered round a colosseum bigger than the one in Rome, in the oasis we have been driven in carriages through drifts of apricot blossom; a barefoot man in loose trousers and a bandana has climbed a coconut palm for us, posing cockily for cameras at the top.

That actress, Judi Dench, got hurt falling off a camel, she persists.

She was in a race, I say. *We won't be doing that.*

Cassie falls silent, watching the increasingly arid countryside.

Perhaps we could drive instead, like we did in the oasis. Don't you think so?

Cassie, I say, startling myself by my commitment, *you may do as you please, but I am definitely riding the camel.*

We have checked in to our hotel and changed, as advised, into loose comfortable trousers; we have been issued with cheap cotton djellabas, to protect our clothes, and kaffiyehs, secured with beaded strings, to keep the sun from our heads. Now we are standing, a crowd of unconvincing extras from *Lawrence of Arabia,* on the ignoble, debris-strewn fringe of the Sahara, apprehensively watching a string of camels come down the road.

Most of the drivers, each of whom leads two beasts, are middle-aged and hirsute, but we are assigned to a much younger man, a thin boy in a ragged djellaba and worn flip-flops. Despite his youth he deals with us with quiet authority, insisting that Cassie, as the taller lady, must ride the bigger camel, settling us solicitously on saddles behind the flaccid, half-empty humps, soothing Cassie's alarm as the beasts lurch disconcertingly to their feet.

However inept you may be on a horse, you are at least contained in the natural hollow of its back. On a camel you have nothing to the rear but the sharp downward declivity of its backside. You are, moreover, mounted above the engine; you roll with every langorous swaying step. In addition, the animals are hot, hairy and smelly, full of strange oaths and colonic rumbles, and prone to unpredictable outbreaks of lust or temper. I apologise silently to Cassie for my persistence.

The camel-leader walks between us, protective, encouraging, and chatty, but standing no nonsense.

She want a man, he explains cheerfully, fetching Cassie's camel a clout when it tries to bite mine in the neck. I nod nervously, Cassie looks appalled. After a little while the rhythm comes easier, I begin to feel I am getting the hang of it, but then the boy breaks into a gentle jog, and the camels quicken their pace. The lurching and swaying increase insufferably, and Cassie actually cries out. He slows down again at once and flashes me a quick grin over his shoulder.

We stop for a while, have cigarette, he says, ordering the camels to kneel. We dismount with relief.

We are barely a quarter-mile from the road, but now the dunes surround us on all sides, dark sculptural masses against the declining sun; gold, amber and rose where the light catches them. I know that the rest of the party cannot be far away, but they are as invisible as if the sand had smothered them. In the universe of shadows and colours there are only the two of us, and the boy tethering the camels.

He looks no more than twenty, with a lightness of bone that makes him seem even younger. His skin is a very dark, matt black, and his features delicate and finely cut. He finds the two of us funny; he looks as if he is suppressing laughter.

You have cigarettes? he says hopefully.

Cassie produces cigarettes and a lighter, a hint of reserve in her manner.

We sit down?

We sit down, on a cloth which he spreads for us on the warm sand, our backs against a dune, he in the middle.

Where you come from?

London, we say.

Ah London. Very big city.

London fails as a topic of conversation: too unimaginable, too indescribable.

You are married ladies?

We both say yes. *My husband died,* I add.

He looks at me, a quick searching glance, and nods.

And you? I say, *Have you got a wife?*

He laughs. *How can I marry? My father is dead. I am oldest of ten brothers and sisters, and I must take care of my mother. I cannot marry for long time.*

One of the camels says something offensive to the other, which retaliates with bared teeth. The boy shouts curses and gets up to readjust the tethers.

Have you any money on you? I ask Cassie. Mine is in the hotel safe.

She looks alarmed. *Do you think we're supposed to tip him?*

I imagine so, don't you? I imagine that's what the family story is all about.

Don't you think it's true, then?

I shrug my shoulders.

The boy comes back, and cadges another cigarette. Cassie is definitely tight-lipped this time. We sit in silence, the boy between us as before, his arms outstretched behind our heads, his hands brushing our shoulders. We watch the shift of colours in the dunes.

Go back now, he says.

He hoists Cassie on to her camel, and returns for me.

Your kaffiyeh no good, he says. *I fix it.*

He stands very close to me to do it, so that our bodies touch lightly from the chest down. He smells of cigarettes and musk, and faintly of camel. I can feel his sex against mine and I suddenly want him closer, I want him inside me. The sand is shifting under my feet and I brace my legs against it, and against the pulse of heat that is pushing me to give way, to let my knees buckle and lean with all my weight against him. He does not look into my eyes but works intently on the string of the head-dress, his expression concentrated and tender, his small hard hands deft, delicately offering his wares, leaving the decision to me.

I can step back, I think, and nothing will have happened. If I step forward instead, everything else will follow: some tactful arrangement will be made at the hotel, such a thing must certainly have happened before. Money will be involved, of course, the boy has his living to earn. I don't mind that, I prefer a simple transaction, satisfaction given on both sides.

Cassie will be aghast, and thrilled; she will certainly gossip. I'll be risking exploitation, infatuation, abuse, disease. So, it occurs to me, will he.

I put my hand on the side of his neck, where it joins his skinny shoulder, and step forward.

Booker Night in Baggot Street

Barry Troy

"Bloody thing's all hype and marketing," Horgan said, disgustedly.

Horgan has a thing about marketing, reckons the civilised world is going down the tubes because of it. Don't mention the name Saatchi in Horgan's company. Anyone'd think the Saatchis have it in for the Horgans way he goes on about them. The Turner Prize is another topic best avoided.

"Last thing the Booker's about is literature," Horgan said.

We wouldn't have started into the subject of books – literature generally – if it hadn't been Booker night and if we weren't sick and tired of talking about political corruption and the scandals with the banks, the way they were all ripping us off.

By that stage, by Booker night, sleaze was coming thick and fast as tribunals of inquiry banged on in Dublin Castle and more and more stones were overturned. Surprise followed surprise as po-faced elder lemons and grey eminences appeared on television scurrying across the cobbles of Castle Yard to spend hours twisting in the wind, inventing a whole new language, as they tried to avoid stringing words into coherent sentences that might incriminate them. It was a first for most of the public to put faces to names, to see at last the guys who really controlled their lives and mortgages. And it was all bad guys – didn't seem to be any shady dolls. What with the bishops in the shit already, it was one hell of a time for male role models.

There was me and Horgan and Cooney in Reilly's and it couldn't have been more than nine in the evening. Tell you how early it was, we were still on pints. I remember that because I was ordering a round the first time yer man put his oar in. Horgan was swearing he was going over to tequila if and when Germaine Greer came on. She's another that's close to the top of the Horgan shit list. I don't know what that poor woman did to his family, but she's one of Horgan's reddest rags.

We were in the public bar where Reilly has the television. Normally we'd have been in the saloon where you could have a conversation at the half-roar setting. Because we were fairly shouting, yer man could overhear what we said. Right then the bar was still glued to *News at Nine* – some woman giving out stink about pollution in Galway Bay, as I recall. We were half-listening to it – Cooney's from Galway and me and Horgan were hoping to get a dig in at some stage, get a rise out of him.

We were at the bar – Horgan facing me, Cooney on the arc between us. Yer man was behind Horgan, kinda crouched over, but without a barstool. He had a pint glass half full of Guinness between his elbows. He had on a herringbone-patterned grey overcoat that looked expensive. It didn't seem the kind of night for an overcoat but I remember thinking the weather could have changed since we came into the pub. He was trying to find his definitive expression in the bar mirror.

First off I didn't think he was talking to us when he spoke. I don't think Horgan heard him and he was nearest although he had his back to him. Horgan was in full flight, giving out shit about having wasted good money on Keri Hulme's *The Bone People* after she'd won the Booker years before.

"Have either of you ever tried it?" Horgan asked. "Unfuckingreadable."

"Hasn't been anything worthwhile since *Midnight's Children*," yer man said, not even turning to us, addressing the mirror.

"What kind of judging is that?" Horgan was asking, not having heard him. "Might as well read the collected edition of the Catholic Herald. Absolute bullshit."

He buried his face in his pint.

"No soul, that's your problem," Cooney said.

"*The God of Small Things* was good, too," yer man said. "Those Indians or Pakis or whatever they are, they know how to write. Say what you will, for a crowd that only stopped using Sanskrit or whatever a few short years ago they do OK." He had the kind of voice that carries without really shouting. I was furthest from him and it came across clear.

"Typical," Horgan said, turning his head, swinging a little on his seat, speaking to yer man in the mirror. "That's the kind of sloppy talk I hate. What in the name o' Christ are short years?"

"Like *The Dubliners* when they started singing back in the sixties," yer man said, ignoring his comment. He drank from his pint. He smeared his mouth with the back of his hand and tried a new expression in the mirror.

That non sequitur caught Horgan, reeled him in. The man couldn't resist it. He swung around and put both hands on the bar counter.

"For Jaysus sake, what do *The Dubliners* have to do with it?"

"The effect they had," yer man said. "No one had ever sung songs like that on radio before."

"This your first day in the pub?" Cooney asked, quite politely I thought.

"Like for example," yer man said, not bothering with Cooney, still talking to his reflection, but looking at Horgan all the same. "Their song 'Seven Drunken Nights' – that was banned at the time, if you remember. Course that was all down to the Church. It wasn't just boys the clergy were interfering with back then. Song was in the British charts at the time."

"Back up, back up," Horgan said. "Christ's sake man, where's all this leading?"

"I remember when I came home from Wolverhampton," yer man went on, not a bit put out, "I was stopped by the customs 'cause I was carrying a copy of *Some Came Running.* Prick thought it was a dirty book. Now, there was a man who could write. James Jones. Made a good film of his other one, *From Here to Eternity*. That caused a stir as well. Burt Lancaster sockin' it to yer woman on the strand. Priest down at home – total wanker – wouldn't allow it to be shown. They wanted to burn it."

"Deborah Kerr," Horgan said. "That's who he was doing it with. I remember it well. Hitchcock used to say give him ice-cold English beauties every time. Man had a point. They say yer woman – ya know the one, Climb Every Mountain – the singer girl? Ya know her – they say she was a favourite of his, go like a rattler in butter."

"Hitchcock didn't do *From Here to Eternity*," Cooney said.

"Did I say he did?" Horgan demanded aggressively.

"Long as you didn't," Cooney said.

"And did you let them take the book?" I asked yer man. "The customs people."

"Course I fuckin' didn't," yer man said. "That a dirty book? the customs fella said. He was about fifty. Big bollix with a Guinness balcony. Depends on the state of yer mind, I said. He started leafing through it, looking for a dirty bit. Prick probably couldn't read. Then the Captain or whatever he's called came up and takes it off him, gives it back to me."

"Who do you fancy tonight?" Horgan asked, calling for pints.

"The South African," yer man says.

"Coetzee?" Cooney says.

"Him," yer man says. "Best of a poor lot. Even though he won it before and no one's ever done it twice. Still I'm glad that thing of Doyle's isn't in. The one about the GPO in 1916. I thought they'd have Salman on the cards again this year. Or the other Paki, Vikram whatever. Suppose we should be grateful for small mercies. Never hear the end of it from U2 if Salman's book won."

"What's yer problem with 1916?" The voice was raucous. The man was so small I missed him the first time I looked behind me. "Roddy Doyle is a fuckin' man of the people, which is more than can be said of the likes of fuckin' youse." Legs wide apart, pint in right hand, left hand on counter to maintain uncertain equilibrium, red face thrust forward, he made his challenge. I stepped away from the counter to give him room, let Horgan and yer man see what they were up against.

"Never said he wasn't," yer man said with considerable aplomb, still looking in the mirror. "Just that I figure Doyle's Henry character has a touch too much magic realism for a subject like the rebellion."

"That's 'cause you don't see the meaning of his father's leg," the little man said.

"Right you are then, Cyril Connolly," Horgan said, pulling his face out of a new pint, froth across his lip. "What do you reckon is the symbolism of his father's wooden leg?"

"Fuck off, youse," the little man said.

He put his pint on the counter and squared up to seated Horgan.

"I know your type," he said. "Fuckin' Tiger Economy bollix. Want everything you see. That's not what men like Pearse and Connolly fought and died for."

"Not what I said at all," Horgan said. "Stick to the fuckin' point. What do you think is the symbolism in Henry's da's wooden leg?"

"Sean O Casey – he could tell ya," the little man said. "There was a true Dub for ya. Born and reared at the Five Lamps."

"In my arse," yer man said. "Doyle is all written out. He just won't fuckin' give up."

"What do youse know?" the little man said. "What do youse know?"

"It's startin'," Cooney said. Cooney loves books.

"Now we'll see who's right," the little man said.

We all looked up at the screen. A thin blond woman with a Scottish accent started talking about books and Bookers to a panel of nondescript characters.

"Ever since *How Late it Was, How Late*" yer man said, "they think you have to have a fuckin' Scottish accent to read books. That and *Trainspotting*."

"Give her a chance," I said. "At least there's no sign of Germaine Greer yet."

"She pisses me off," the little man said.

"For once I agree with ya," Horgan said.

"If you two are finished bonding could we watch the fuckin' programme," a big man at a table said.

We all swung about. He looked like he could back it up so we turned round again.

Members of the panel were suggesting books they reckoned should have been up.

"You think Toibin has a chance?" Cooney asked, speaking to the mirror.

"Nah," the little man said. He took a bite out of a fresh pint.

I ordered tequilas, seemed like a good idea.

"Ja read it?" Horgan asked.

"No need to," the little man said. "Know the kind of thing Toibin writes. Lotta people down the country navel gazin'. Searching for the lost child in themselves. Fuck 'em. Didn't like that last one of his either. Only got to page ten then I gave up."

"I tried reading *Anna Karenina* four times and never got past page fifty," I said.

"Wha'!" the little man said. "Mean to tell me you never finished Dostoyevsky's masterpiece?"

"He didn't write it," Horgan said.

The little man was incensed.

"Typical," he said, "fuckin' typical. Air-brushed outa history! What do youse know?"

"I know he didn't write it," Horgan said.

"There's yer man, Victor Paxman," the little man said.

"Melvyn Bragg ya mean," Horgan said, "and Dostoyevsky still didn't write it."

"That's a rug," the little man said. "Natural hair won't stand up like that."

Melvyn started telling us what the guests were having for dinner.

"That's Anita Desai," Cooney said, as the camera panned about amongst the diners.

"Fuck me, here come the Indians," yer man said.

"A ton of an improvement on your woman with *Green Plums*," Cooney said, "and she picked up a cool hundred grand from our lot. I don't see Salman."

"That's 'cause he's not there," Horgan said.

A good-looking youngish woman came into the bar. She had a determined walk. Whatever it was that brought her in she'd made her mind up, that was for sure. She halted the other side of Cooney and spoke to the back of yer man's head.

"Are you comin' home?" she said, and there was a sudden hush.

It was just like that part in *Shane* where he goes into the bar for the lemonade.

He didn't turn around. He watched her in the mirror.

"Will ya have something?" he asked her, his voice not unreasonably loud.

"Did ya hear me? Are you comin' home?" she said.

"I'm watching the Booker Prize," he said, enouncing it a bit preciously if you ask me.

She stared at him in the mirror for a few moments. We could all sense that was a straw too many. She flicked back her coat, put her hands on her hips, threw back her head.

"Oh, excuse me," she said. "I didn't realise. Jesus I'm sorry. I mean if I'd known you were watching the Booker Prize I wouldn't have got the bus in here. Wouldn't have spent an hour and a half looking for a babysitter. I mean, Jesus, the Booker Prize! The fuckin' Booker. Are you or are you not coming home? Last fuckin' time."

"You're in a public place," he said, without turning.

Analysing it afterwards we all agreed he said it with simple dignity, but he might have put it better.

She looked about in a kind of astonished desperation before picking up the nearest thing to her, which happened to be the fresh pint of the big man at the table.

She threw it at the back of yer man's head. Fair play to her, she could throw a pint. She hit him spot on and the glass broke. Some of the stout shot up onto the screen. We lost definition and Melvyn went all blurry.

She turned on her heel and walked out.

The big man had to hit someone, so he belted yer man and coolly demanded a replacement pint as he straddled the fallen body.

Yer man pulled himself together and stood up.

"The bloody bitch," he said, when he realised the big man was genuinely very big.

He lurched out the door.

Reilly took a cloth and began cleaning the television after he'd turned it off.

We heard the squeal of brakes and the blast of a klaxon in the road outside. I think we all knew then it was yer man. Cooney went out and was gone about ten minutes.

"Was it him?" the little man asked.

"Yeah," Cooney said, and threw back a tequila. "Taken away in an ambulance. Wouldn't give ya much for his chances. Who won the Booker?"

Cooney really loves books.

Postcard from New York

Tom Murray

Woke up this morning to something you never get in this city.

Silence.

Not a car horn, siren, or murmur of voices reaching up to the 14th floor.

The street below was empty or so I thought. In the flats opposite the hotel folk were also looking down from windows to the street below.

Then I saw what they saw.

A road block of police cars and then a figure like an extra out of a B movie moving slowly up the street. He or she was dressed in what looked like a deep sea diving suit. He or she walked slowly, very slowly.

I followed his, or her every slow step until they stopped and I saw it. Directly across from my hotel was a briefcase, an everyday briefcase, sitting upright, and so alone looking, on the sidewalk.

And I was on the 14th floor with a lift I had already found out never arrived when you wanted it.

I watched.

The deep sea diver with what looked like a metal rod ever so slowly edged open the case (I don't know how that suit would have protected him) and out flew ... paper. Paper that drifted higher and higher down the street, to God knows where else.

Minutes later the car horns, sirens, murmur of voices returned and folk streamed, almost bored looking, out of flats and hotels like water released from a dam.

And I walked down the fourteen flights of stairs and joined them.

Love to the boys.

How to Kill a Latin Teacher

Caroline Koeppel

It wasn't so surprising that Nathan McCormick suggested, passing the pasta bowl to his left, that perhaps it was time to put the Latin teacher out of her misery, but that, despite reading only English translations all year long, he attempted to say it in some form of Latin.

"Tomorrow pugnare Miss Blankenhaus."

This was most impressive to the other boys since McCormick had been a mere last minute fill-in for one senior who fell sick before the annual Honors Latin trip to Italy.

They were on the tenth day now, having started in Rome to trace a twelve-day journey of Dido and Aeneas. Mr. Tortelli, a lifetime assistant until Blankenhaus' demise, was along to step in at times when a woman couldn't. He hardly shared Blankenhaus' enthusiasm for retracing dead people's steps, and in a private moment, out of range of Blankenhaus' good ear, told the boys that the most important things in life boiled down to sex.

Perhaps it did and McCormick knew that. Blankenhaus was nearing seventy. Never married, no children – she was, he convinced the other boys, rather superfluous both in the department and out.

The boys, all six of them, at dinner in proper Collegiate attire – navy blazer and solid tie, even in the wilds of Italy, agreed that McCormick had a point but that, in fact, he was not the best man for the job. Really, Arthur Quigley was better suited, as he was underweight, frail and the highest scorer on the SATs. No one would suspect him. Blankenhaus even favored Quigley, had a thing for him really, and hoped he would go on to Princeton to be a classics major. Little did she know that after Quigley saw the Princeton Latin Club in fitted-sheet togas, dancing around a New

Jersey maple, that come finals he was through with Catullus, and his bound copies of Ovid's *Metamorphoses* volumes I and II would be tossed in the cafeteria trash.

The boys thought Quigley should sidle up to Blankenhaus at dessert, so that he could get a fuller grasp of her proportions. As he approached her from behind, her round cheeks filled with color, and she swept her blue tinted wisps away from her forehead.

"Ah," Blankenhaus said, beaming to Tortelli. "Puer Icarus Una Stabat."

It was a story – Blankenhaus' all time favorite – which she loved to recount of the boy who with wings made out of feathers and wax, dropped from the sky as he came too near the sun that melted the whole mess.

Quigley obediently translated in a lifeless manner, "The boy Icarus was standing alone." Though he could hardly give a flying Icarus that this gave Blankenhaus immediate and enormous pleasure.

"Sit, sit, Mr. Quigley, please." She patted the empty chair next to her. Beside her plate she and Tortelli had laid out maps and schedules that planned out every mile and minute of the next day's events. They would drive from Sorrento back to Rome in the evening, but first they would visit the Island of Capri.

"Capri," Tortelli read aloud, "is an island with no crime."

"Imagine that," Blankenhaus said wistfully. "Unfortunately, not like our island of Manhattan."

"Well," McCormick reported in a late night bedroom conference, the boys smartly dressed in flannel pajamas, "Capri is our only chance." Because didn't it make sense, he explained to the others, that a crime committed on an island without crime would most likely go undetected? Those Capricians would be ill prepared to handle it, being out of practice.

"And to change all those tour books," Howard Marcus said, always one step behind and wearing a nightshirt. "They'd never do it."

If Blankenhaus knew it was her last day, she never let on. However, Tortelli seemed oddly a bit tense. The boys enthusiastically complimented Miss Blankenhaus on her thin paisley blouse and skirt, fought over the seat next to her on the bus, and recited odes passionately into her good ear. Meanwhile Quigley worked out the logarithms of the chair lift that would take them over Capri. He drew diagrams and seating arrangements, showing one boy at a time their plan of action, all sketched neatly out in the last page of a pocket-sized Latin dictionary.

"There, you see, that dip in the parabola, the U of the ride, would be the best place for Blankenhaus to make her exit."

There is little to say what causes a boy to go from good to bad. Did Quigley have parents who bought him nice clothes and pay for his education? He did. Was Mrs. Quigley pleased to tell her friends that her son had turned down Harvard and Yale? She was. And didn't Mr. Quigley already own a Princeton trashcan, tie, belt and shot glass, complete with Tiger and motto? Of course.

But Arthur Quigley felt that they never really loved him, so much as the idea of him. He had merely completed a picture. Their detachment incited in him a strong neediness and longing, so that he was always striving to be the best at everything in order to win some sort of unattainable approval. Only after a brief stint in summer camp did Arthur realize his efforts were futile. He had written many long, flowery, metaphoric letters to his parents, worthy he thought of at least posthumously being published, and prolifically well beyond the mandatory two pages a week. And in return? As he raced with the other boys to the mailroom each day at 3 p.m., he could push his hand clear through the cubby without interference. They had sent him nothing.

There was, of course, only one explanation. His parents must have been killed in one of those bizarre Circle Line cocktail cruise accidents, where someone drunkenly drops off the back of the boat – while everyone else is piled up at the front getting a closer look at the Statue of Liberty.

At night without the distractions of whiffle-ball and kayaking, Quigley could imagine the whole thing as if he had been there. His mother going over first, with the swan-like grace of a Mexican cliff-diver, then his father more awkwardly making his way one trousered leg at a time over the rail, holding his nose, then jumping heroically to rescue Mrs. Quigley from being sucked into the blades of the motor.

But Arthur Quigley, having been taught to be strong in the face of any tragedy, preferred not to alert the camp's authorities; it was his duty to remain stoical and carry forth. And this he could do respectably well. When, one day, the kleptomaniacal camp counselor discovered there was no illicit candy to take from Quigley's trunk, asked with mock concern where the hell were Quigley's parents anyway, he merely pointed skyward with an angelic expression and answered tragically, "Up there."

After a brief investigation by the camp director, and only three weeks remaining, a letter soon arrived, typed by Mr. Quigley's secretary and cc'ed to him in the lower left corner.

Dear Son,

Having a good summer. Went sailing yesterday. Tonight will eat corn.

All the best,

Your Father

This was all Quigley needed to confirm his worst suspicions. No one living who knew him and loved him could write such a letter, lacking in details and warmth and, of course, a personal pronoun. But then, three weeks later, oddly enough, there they were, darkly tanned and somewhat trimmer; his long lost parents, waiting for him in the parking lot with a six pack of bananas.

It was this strange detachment Quigley now possessed – the carapace of his personality clearly attributable at the very least to the camp incident – that deftly and not regrettably allowed him to keep others at a distance. He didn't dislike Miss Blankenhaus, but he didn't care for her either. Wasn't it Mr. Tortelli who said the opposite of love was not hate but disinterest? Yes. And now, when he closed his eyes and suddenly pictured her gone, he felt nothing more than slight dizziness and fatigue. Blankenhaus, noticing that Quigley's eyes were suddenly shut, worried that he might be malnourished and feeling weak; she hastily rummaged her fleshy pink hands through the debris of her oversized purse in the hope of unearthing a mashed Tootsie Roll.

While she searched, the other five boys and Mr. Tortelli loaded themselves onto the chairlift and Blankenhaus gave them all a quick disinterested wave.

"We'll be right behind you."

There were eight empty chairs ahead of them and no one in line behind by the time Blankenhaus settled on a cherry LifeSaver, a dusty and dried up spare, in lieu of the Tootsie.

"Come Mr. Quigley," she said, and clamped onto his elbow as the operator slowed the chair enough to swoop them up from behind.

The initiation of Quigley's life of crime brought back scenes of Blankenhaus over the years in brief vignettes like a quick documentary of her achievements. Once she had pulled him roughly by the ear from his chair when he had forgotten to do his declensions, reminding him as she ran first slowly then quicker through them herself, "A... Ae... A... Ae, Ae... Arum, Am... As, A... Is," that they were, in fact, the sounds of love; a woman having an orgasm. And then there were the repetitive instances of dissecting the word 'assume' on the board. "Remember Quigley", she was fond of saying, "when you ASSUME, you make an ASS out of U and ME."

The trip up the grassy hill was just as Quigley had diagrammed. For a brief few yards the high weeds brushed the bottoms of their shoes, then the lift gained momentum, and a valley suddenly spread and dropped below them, spotted with yellow flowers and toy-like houses. There was a strong brisk wind picking up across the Mediterranean that swayed the chairs from left to right forcing Blankenhaus to grip the pole more firmly on her left.

"Funny," she said, "there's no protective bar in front of us."

It was funny Quigley thought, and it suddenly seemed more a temptation just to step off himself rather than go to the trouble of removing Blankenhaus.

But no, he had a mission, and the other boys would be disappointed if she was still with him when they landed. His alibi was well prepared – Blankenhaus had forgotten her sunglasses on the bus and would join up with them later back at the hotel. That would leave Capri's crime record nicely intact, the least Quigley could do for the Italians.

The pivotal moment was fast approaching before they would begin their descent and it occurred to Quigley that it might be appropriate if not decent to have Blankenhaus recite Dido's final words to Aeneas as some sort of gesture at a eulogy. But with the whistling gusts and the creaking of the chairs, her good ear on the far side of her head, Blankenhaus only picked up a thin thread of Quigley's request and was veering rapidly off on her own tangent.

"Yes," she nodded turning to look into Quigley's eyes. "A terrible death to be burned at the stake. A horrendous conflagration."

Although Quigley had memorized every word in *30 Days to a Better Vocabulary*, he had just as soon forgotten them. He returned her nod knowingly now, thinking she was referring to some ancient holiday.

Below the razor edge of boulders rose steadily toward them (remnants of the glaciers, she reminded him), and Quigley with no more anxiety than before he swatted a fly, reached his left hand behind Blankenhaus in an effort to shove her off.

Blankenhaus, however, was more solid than he had estimated and his hand swiftly slipped between her blouse and skirt, and, the elastic on her girdle having rotted years before, his palm slid in the fashion of the silver slope of a shoe horn, down between the powdered mounds of her buttocks.

Perhaps Quigley had expected a sensation of disgust if he was capable of feeling anything at all, but instead a tremor that started it seemed in the tassels of his loafers, traveled instantly up his knees in a wave of electrocution and settling just beneath the zipper of his khakis, he had to catch his breath.

Blankenhaus speaking mid-sentence, stopped, a cloudy unfocused quality taking over her silver blue eyes. Her lips quivered slightly then turning upward in a lopsided grin, she sighed softly, and reaching behind her, pushed Quigley's hand even further, but not before whispering, "Alea iacta est," and translating breathlessly herself, grazed her bright pink lips against his earlobe. "The die is cast."

Only now as they reached the point in their descent where the others grew magically from blazer-ed specks to bored boys and one Mr. Tortelli, waving dismally from the platform at the sight of them both, did Blankenhaus remove Quigley from beneath her skirt, and place his hand rather sensitively over his crotch.

There was no explanation demanded and none that Quigley could offer upon landing and dutifully helping Blankenhaus move her blue head quickly out of the swerving chairs' way, except that his calculations were slightly off and clearly another boy would have to do the job.

In what was perceived by Mr. Tortelli as a mature pensiveness that had newly taken over Quigley, no doubt awed by the scenery and magnitude of their journey, he patted him hard on the blazer-ed back as they meandered through the narrow streets with the others. McCormick was now working out the calculations himself, disgusted that a boy with almost perfect math skills could screw up a murder, but Quigley, immune in his own world, lagged slowly behind. Every garlic scented breeze or roar of a muffler was potent and fresh to his senses. Colors and sensations reached a heightened and high-pitched vibrancy; Quigley stopped frequently now to linger at each stall, irresistibly drawn to its treasures. If only to caress now the velvety brown fur of a rabbit foot charm, to fondle the lush down of an angora sweater, thinking only and longingly of the voluptuous, divided magnitude of dear Miss Blankenhaus' bottom and the powerful wonder of a dead language.

Believe It

Brian Tiernan

"Bless me Father for I have sinned ... its 4 weeks since my last confession."

"Yes my son."

"I cursed 32 times, Father."

"I took the Lord's Name in vain 28 times."

"I gave backchat to my mother 8 times."

"I gave backchat to my father once."

"Carry on my son."

"I had bad thoughts 56 times, Father."

"Did you abuse yourself?"

Fingers crossed.

"What do you mean?"

"Did you pull your wire ... play with your mickey?"

"Certainly not."

"Good lad ... you'll go blind and lose your hair."

Through the confessional gauze I can see Father Doocey's bald head and milk bottle glasses.

"Anything else?"

"I felt a girl Father."

"Inside or outside her clothes?"

"Outside ... I think she was a Protestant."

"Thank God for that ... what age are you gosson?"

"13½"

"Stay away from dirty women and girls ... your mickey will rot and fall off."

"I will Father ..."

Fingers loosed.

"*In nomine patria ...*"

"I'm not finished yet, Father."

"Yes, sonny?"

"I robbed my granny's shop 20 times."

"What did you rob?"

"Bulls eyes ... nancy balls ... the odd 10 Gold Flake ... the price of the pictures."

"Any money?"

"*No.*"

"It's not a sin to steal off your relatives."

Believe it!

"For your penance ... say a decade of the Rosary for the conversion of Russia ... Joe Stallion died last month ... the joyful mysteries."

Out the door into the Easter Saturday mid-day sunshine.

Can't wait to tell my pal Tonto what the priest said about robbing your relatives.

His uncle has a pub in Connaught Street.

Beirut-Paris-Beirut

Selma Dabbagh

My grandmother said nobody could do enough to protect me from the evil eye. My beauty was unsuited to my birth. My frivolity unsuited to my circumstances and my gender. The fact that I longed for Paris when brought up in a refugee camp in West Beirut shows the folly of my youth. I used to dream of men in dark suits bearing flowers. Imagine. The residue of such reverie haunts and mocks. I cannot dislodge it. It has defined me and written my sorry fate.

But now I am about to actually make it to Paris, albeit on the wrong side of forty and for a conference rather than a lover. I am travelling with my silent colleague Zaid and the conference is, again, on us. The world's oldest refugees. The suited and booted of us representing the naked and the barefoot.

Clamped into my foam and metal plane seat I know I am fated for another one of life's sick jokes. He is coming, all covered in official glory. It's twenty-three years since I last saw him. A late addition to the list of speakers, he is supposed to substitute Professor Hafiz who has been denied an exit visa from the West Bank to attend.

The picture of Paris I saw as a girl, I had found in a magazine thrown out of one of the aid workers' apartments in the camp. The magazine mainly had pictures of girls with short hair and plastic earrings who looked either angry or sad. The page said 'Paris is for Lovers,' and had some photos of hotels. The picture itself was an old one, in black and white, of two figures; a woman being bent backwards by a man who is kissing her. There is a feeling he is in a hurry, he has a bicycle in the other hand, but he cannot resist. She has been pulled into it by him and there is an old man watching. What I liked the most was the feeling that she did not care.

The picture made my stomach feel soft and excited so I had torn it out, folded it square and kept it under the cover of my mattress so it did not show when we rolled them up in the morning.

My airport bus window shows me that not everyone is kissing in Paris. The city is full of busy bureaucrats prepared for a flood. The rain relentlessly slides over slate overcoats and collects in worn paving stones. Paris is only partly for lovers. It's mainly for workers and bright, spoilt children all covered in colour.

He is there when we walk into the hotel lobby. His posse of middle sized, middle aged Middle Easterners is standing at ease. Smoke circles their heads like the cartoon Mexican's flies. The squat horse-shoe arrangement is left open at the front to allow those in it to look out. To vet those who enter, as Zaid and I do, sodden with dark Paris rain, dragging bags of pamphlets and petitions.

His name is Mazen Hadidi and I met him in a Red Crescent hospital in Beirut in 1981. He had been injured in the fighting and I was responsible for bedpans and bandages on his floor. I was 17 and he was older and he was funny. I say he was older, but still he was young, he could only have been 22 or 24. He had huge dark eyes that could swim with intrigue and pop with emphasis. He told stories and jokes that had patients giggling through air raids. They moved their beds closer to his and fought over who would be next to him. The walking came from other wards to hover at the door, double up on beds and pull nurses' chairs around him.

His stories. They went like this. They were about three soldiers, one from a town, Ibn Madan, another from a village, Ibn Fellah and the third a Bedouin, Ibn Bedu. These soldiers had met each other as boys in the catastrophe of '48 and then they meet again in the victory of Karamah in 1968; they go on to fight in Black September in 1970 and then form a militia under the PLO's Fateh in Beirut. He tells us that he has just left them and he will return to them once he can walk again. The hero changes in each story. Ibn Madan is the intellectual with family connections and knowledge of the outside world. Ibn Fellah knows nature, weather and has common sense. Ibn Bedu is stubborn, loyal and determined. More importantly, he also understands the stars. These men pull together not just to fight, but also to find food, to help each other with their family troubles and when they fall sick in love as they do so frequently.

When he told these stories, Mazen Hadidi used to sometimes look up at me during a pause or when there were questions from his audience or statements of exasperation at the folly of one of the brigade. And I was as captivated by him as everyone was.

Flying over Hungary, Zaid orders a brandy; "I used to drink it with my aunt, in Syria," he says, responding to my raised eyebrows, "... a communist. You should have one too." We have finished the spreadsheets of refugee numbers and ages, devised a neat flow chart to show the reasons behind the declining educational and health standards. We have crossed-checked references. We bring with us the agreed draft resolution we seek approval for. We have two more hours to Paris. If Zaid is happy to stop working, then so am I. I agree to the plastic cup of gold liquid. I am not a drinker. I test it on my tongue. My eyes water. So, Zaid has a communist aunt? It must be one of the only things Zaid has ever told me of his family although we have worked back-to-back for over five years now. After the first week together I had detected in him a total aversion, if not contempt, for small talk and never pursued it. Neither did he. So we stuck to work and there was enough of that for ten of us.

So when he says "Nawal" I am grateful when he also says "my wife" because I am not sure I would have recognised her name. "Nawal is now in the Gulf, with the children."

"She has family there?" I ask

"Yes ... and she will be re-marrying there." He laughs a little awkwardly and I think, hell, that is more than I asked for and want to get right out of the conversation and the brandy right then and there. But it would involve climbing over his lap or asking him to stand and the toilets have red lights shining "Engaged-Engaged." Ridiculous. I panic. He is not going to, what do the Americans call it? He's not going to hit on me is he?

"I am sorry, I did not realise you were ..."

"No, it's all quite new. It's been coming for a while though. A bad marriage made in war I guess. In fact, in truth, we never really had any interest in each other what so ever." He measures out the last three words with care and lets them drop out individually, "what-so-ever" he repeats. He smiles with relief at having said them.

"The children?"

"Except the children and that's where it hurts. You know with children, you don't ...?"

I shake my head in an exaggerated way. How could he not know? I thought it was all people knew about me. But him almost suggesting that I could have some or had some or that it is almost inconsequential – it is like a space opening up in front of me.

"They are, they are, my heart, I feel their pain before I feel my own. But they are old enough to travel now so I should see them several times a year and they need their mother more than I, so it's for the best that they are with her."

One of the toilets is no longer engaged. I could go now. The plane drops into an air pocket. The *Fasten Your Seat Belts* sign is switched on. Turbulence. I am skating around in my silent head. It's too rude to go back to talking about work.

"Have you met, the man ... the one she will marry?"

"Yes, I have. He is, you know ... nice. Devoted to her, a little older, a widower." He thinks for a while. "Rich."

"It helps," I suggest. He finds this amusing.

"It certainly does help her."

"And they met in the Gulf?"

"No, here – Beirut, he was on holiday and needed a suit."

"A suit?"

"She works for the Raoufs' tailoring business. Haute Couture in Verdun is the shop. Haute Couture." The name is new and absurd in his mouth. "He bought many suits that summer apparently. Many."

"Well attired then?"

"Very well attired."

"At least now I can do my job in peace. She hated what I do, well what we do. Thought it was degrading to spend so much time in the camps. She could not bear to be reminded that I came from them ..."

Over Austria we ask for two more of the same.

I remember one of the doctors, the one with the drooping eyes, cigarettes and moustache, Doctor Khalaf, saying, "He saves more lives than I do, together with his little trio: Mazen Hadidi the Sheherazade of Ward Three." Mazen was Sheherazade but in reverse, he used suspense to save their lives, not his. The elixir of anticipation he concocted through the amputation of his stories spread through the hospital. He left his audience hanging with Abu Fellah in the fields, his Kalashnikov in the well, enemy troops approaching. Abu Bedu's desperate love for Ibn Madan's sister frustrated by her father.

"Shame on you!" would be the screams across the ward, "you can't just stop right there." But he would. Prop up the cushions, sometimes give me a wink, light a cigarette and let them protest around him. "Well if you can't tell us the end, tell us the beginning again," and so it would start again. And the details. Like my grandmother with the details, he would not lose any. Exactly the same the second time around. And the third. "You are a stupid generation," my grandmother would tell me, "you push to write everything down and read everything later so you have nothing left in your heads."

"Do you know Mazen Hadidi?" I ask Zaid as we cross into Germany, and immediately wish I hadn't.

"The Deputy Minister? Of course I know of him. I can't say I have ever met him. Why?"

"No reason. He is speaking instead of Professor Hafiz."

"I saw the message. Strange choice."

"How so?"

"Well maybe not," Zaid pulls down the plastic glass holder, traces his finger around its edge and places his brandy cup in it, "capitulation is, after all, the only solution."

One of the hospital's generators had been bombed in the raid the night before so we coasted along with the other. We rationed our electricity to operating theatres and surrounding corridors. Wards were candle lit. The loss of the second generator was announced by a judder, a blast and a gigantic dust-cloth falling over the building.

Mazen finds me in the corridor and calls my name. I'm surprised that he's walking. The corridor's moonlit. Dark boxes grow and shrink in their shadows, silver smudges glitter on the walls' paint gloss. "Put it down." He waves smiling at the towels in my hand. “Follow me,” his finger against his lips and he looks so mischievous, I thought he was going to play a trick on the other patients. He takes my hand and leads me down the corridor. I am so excited. Mazen Hadidi is holding my hand.

I have replayed the next ten or so minutes so many times in my memory that I have worn down the grooves between my recollections. I spin from being thrust into the heap of dirty bedding under the stairs to seeing the dark liquid curling between my legs. There is a repeat groove over and over again where his nicotine cavern of a mouth is covering mine with desperate breath. I see the photo of the Paris couple for a second and realise that it is now happening. There is a tear in me. Glass splinters being pushed inside. I gasp. I had said ‘no’ when he touched me but there is a new urge. It is the warmth of showering under hot water after many cold muddy days. I tilt my head back to bask in it. I rest in the pleasure of it. There are stars running down under my skin, grenades exploding in my head, heat glowing between my legs. I am between watery blue compartments and need to get from one to the next for release and he is trying too. He grunts. He whimpers like a child. He can help me to get there so I am pushing him onto me and pleading with him to get through the next barrier. But he stops too fast. My heart is palpitating sick blood in me like after a close gunshot. It is cold and wet down there and he is wiping his face with his sleeve as though recovering from a shock.

You see, I could have stopped him when his hand strayed down the back of my uniform trousers and fumbled with the nappy pin that kept the waistband tight around me. I could have pushed him away when he pulled at his pyjama bottoms to unbutton his flies. I could have said ‘no’ the whole time and maybe he would have stopped but I did not do those things. The girl who has been staring down on the scene from somewhere close the ceiling, hovering like a vapour for twenty-three years tells me I did not do those things. I put my head back for him and I have been punished for having done so. My destiny is now different than it would have been.

In the peak of our tipsiness Zaid and I go as far as saluting each other’s health and failed marriages but the bottled camaraderie wears off as the plane descends into France and we dip back into our own worlds. I make sure the glasses are disposed of, the miniatures gone, my teeth brushed, my breath fresh so there is no trace of alcohol on me before we clip back our seat belts for Charles de Gaulle.

The hotel lobby is low ceilings, squat chandeliers. Finger-print smeared gilt edges. Mazen steps forward to greet us when we enter as though it is his own private residence. His daughter's wedding perhaps? He calls to me with my first name and tests my maiden name as if to say, so it still applies does it? And I am nodding like a child. "You have come so far," he says, "I have heard all about you and your organisation, and I understand you have an ..." his smile is benevolent, "*interesting* resolution to put forward for us to discuss." He has a blue blazer with bronze buttons. It looks very Colonial to me; like a croquet player or a boatman. I ask him whether he had any problems getting through the airport.

"Not too bad, really, pretty smooth, all things considered."

I introduce Zaid, "Mazen Hadidi, Zaid Yousef."

"Ah." Mazen says when he hears Zaid's surname. "Dr. Yousef is a good friend of mine, a very good friend."

"We are not related." Zaid has gone back to his sober self; a man of short sentences and long pauses. Even Mazen seems somewhat disconcerted. "I am from a different family. Peasants."

"Ibn Fellah!" Mazen smiles and gives me a wink.

Zaid excuses himself and I follow him to reception. I know my hands are shaking even before I try to get my passport out.

My grandmother found out what was wrong with me months later. My breasts had been feeling as though they were pumped with hot mercury. I could barely lower my arms. I had this sense that I had stood up too quickly when hungry although I was eating like a rat. I was forever peeing. The other nurses thought I had taken up smoking and was just making excuses to go to the bathroom all the time. My grandmother had been watching me closely, then one day she just poked me in the chest and when I screamed in agony she swore. At God, the Zionists, the Hospital and All Men. She asked who had done it to me and I was not sure what she could mean. She asked if I had been near a man and I said in the hospital I am always near men as it's my job and I thought it could be something I had picked up from a bed pan. I did think of Mazen but that was a secret thing and I saw no need to tell her. She asked when I had last bled and I couldn't remember. She said I needed a doctor and I said maybe I could talk to Dr. Khalaf, although he is always so busy and she said that I would talk to no one. She dressed, put on her shoes, took some money from the jam jar behind the mattresses, told me to get my coat and almost pushed me out of the house.

I wanted to leave the Paris hotel room almost as soon as I arrived in it. A container of stale breath, sweat and cigarettes, the central heating ground out acid air and shuddered with intestinal discomfort. Tablet sized soaps slapped on ceramic sinks, anonymous greeting cards in multiple languages, mass-produced bedspreads washed and worn of all colouration.

Dislodge your dream of an intimate Paris room. Forget the introduction by the owner's wife, patting down the bed as you arrive. Forget the small vase of pansies.

I decide to go out. The rainy air could cleanse my head as it has the town. I find Zaid standing in the lobby, clumsy with an umbrella.

"They are going to try and stop us," he says nodding in the direction of Mazen's group who are walking towards the dining room, "with the resolution."

"I know, but we anticipated that."

"It makes me sick. They sell us out at every opportunity so that they don't rock the boat at the negotiating table. Not that they are delivering anything." He stops, "I didn't realise you knew him? Mazen Hadidi."

"Oh, from a long time ago. '81."

"I see. I am going to try and find an internet café so I can try and do this video conferencing with my children. You?"

"Just walking." We leave the hotel together. The road puddles swim with eely reflections of streetlights. We walk in silence and I leave him by an internet point filled with backpackers and porn watchers. I dawdle by the Seine trying to block out the sounds of American tourists.

My grandmother had taken me to a part of the town where I had never been. Behind sandbags and riddled buildings. Soldiers jeered at us. I remember some children jumping out in front of me with a toy gun and screaming. Stupid Girl. Says Grandmother. Stupid Girl. I had always been her favourite. We were walking into the gunfire rather than away from it but I could get no explanation from her. She would not talk to me. She just swore.

She took me to a ladies' salon on the inside of a building that had lost its shoulders. There were no customers. The madame had false eyelashes and a loose scarf covering curlers, lipstick seeping around her mouth and over her cigarettes. Her eyes did not move from me.

My grandmother addressed her courteously and I could not imagine how she would know or know of such a woman. The madame hardly saw my grandmother. She told me to stand and pushed at my stomach and fondled my breasts and told my grandmother it was too late for her "remedy," she would need the doctor. Her feet slopped across the room in plastic sandals and I could feel her looking at me from the back, too. She called a scrap of a girl from the inside stairwell to fetch the doctor and returned with an ashtray of flat salted *bizer* seeds that she cracked between her teeth. She put out her hand to my grandmother for payment for the "treatment" and pushed the notes into her bra.

They took me to a room where there was no bed. A large glass covered desk with an alabaster name-plate with decorative Arabic writing declaring a name of a man. It did not say Doctor. "We can't have a bed, you understand, because of the authorities," and I remember thinking "What authorities?" I lay back on the glass and they stripped me from the waist down. I could see through a hole in the wall where a round fan once was, a man on a balcony smoking an argeela.

The doctor had a bag of cold metal, yellowing teeth and a small crucifix around his neck. He said something about us being from the camps to the madame and she nodded, blew smoke out of either side of her mouth and carried on staring. He said something about a new sniper position being set up on the opposite roof and she nodded again, blew more smoke and felt my legs.

The pain was unconscionable. I had been concentrating on dealing with the agony of being so exposed and the shame of having just an old sheet across my stomach and bare legs for everyone to see. But when he used his metal I went into a state of howling shock. I could see the man on the balcony staring right at me then someone hit me around the face and I must have blacked out. The Doctor had gone when I came to. I had huge pads in my panties. And before we left Madame told Grandmother saying she should ask her if she needed me to earn some extra money as I was "quite the type". Outside the building, Grandmother sat behind a sandbag and cried. No one had ever seen my grandmother cry. I had to pull her up and along the road for I was so scared of the sniper in the opposite building.

And if that was the end of it, it may not have been the end of me as a woman, but I developed an infection. It could have been because they had left some cotton inside me that fell out later when I went to the bathroom. Or it could have been because the metal was not clean. They could not tell, but it had gone deep within and they had to gut me like a chicken. They removed all my reproductive gizzards until I was as hollow as a Russian doll.

Mazen says, "May I?" with false courtesy and sits next to me as I finish my breakfast. His eyes twinkle with middle-aged flirtation. "You know I often think of those days, the hospital, you know, I often miss those days."

"How is the Authority treating you?" I ask. I will not finish my coffee as my hands cannot do it.

"Oh, good, good. I am being transferred here, you know, as Representative. It's a good move."

"Yes, well, Paris."

"Yes, fantastic city. Wonderful. I always enjoy coming back. You are familiar with it?"

"It's my first time here."

"No! Impossible! I will take you around, show you things: the Louvre, Notre Dame."

"Let's see how the conference goes."

"I think it will go well. Listen, your Resolution, we have some concerns that it may, you know, not have the right impact at the moment, we are at such a sensitive stage in our negotiations. We really need to build trust."

"It's a basic statement of our position." He gives me a look that says *I know you, don't try to be something different,* so I look away from him to continue the old patter that I know so well, "It is backed by the Representatives of the camps and is no more than a restatement of previous United Nations resolutions. To keep it changes nothing. To compromise it would be –" I use Zaid's word, "outright capitulation."

He smiles at me. The look changes to *my haven't you come a long way* and *you really are quite attractive when you're angry*. I keep staring at him until his expression changes to a *maybe I should move on to another subject.*

"So I heard that you married? A good man, I met him once. You have children?"

There are our organisation's pamphlets on the table. Photos of the refugee children at the new nursery, I smooth my hand over their faces. I know some of them well, and their brothers and sisters.

"These are my children."

Again the smile, "I have four you know, two here in Europe, two back with their mother." He folds his napkin. "You know, I do remember hearing that you had some medical problems after I last saw you. Nasty business I heard. I don't suppose it is public knowledge though. So forgive me for mentioning it."

I am ashamed to be feeling nauseous and shaky again by the time Zaid arrives.

My husband left me because I lied. I not only did not tell him relevant information, that I could not have children, but I also pretended that I could. I loved him desperately. I loved the line of his profile, the movement of his shoulders when he walked, the way he peeled oranges creating one long golden ringlet. He was not from the camps and that made things difficult but we cared for nothing except each other so we jettisoned our families. I knew it was a matter of time until I was found out, but I still carried on making a show of sanitary towels and occasionally spoke of being late when he started getting anxious for children. But I was discovered by another man, a highly recommended specialist, who placed me on a slab and found there was nothing inside; "It is impossible," he told my husband, "that your wife even menstruates."

Where to go when your husband closes the door to you? You are not the woman I married, he said. Where to go when your family have closed the door on you? You are not our daughter, they said. At the time there was one small shelter, which consisted of nothing more than a couple of spare rooms in a flat. Mona's flat. Mona whom they all talked about for her hard face and male voice. They spoke about her more when she died. "She liked women," they said, as though it was a disease. But it is through her I got my work and my life.

I am one of the first speakers after the dignitaries file out into the hall filled with its heroic murals. Zaid sits behind me. The wallpaper of our slides is the face of Nada, only one of the millions of refugees, but chosen because she is a pretty one, cream skinned, coloured eyes. Suffering must be packaged attractively. I can see Mazen joking with his colleagues as I start. I am talking too fast for the interpreter, 'Slow Down Please,' says a message. Breathe, take the slides one by one. I look straight at him. I look at the slide, the audience, but mainly at Mazen Hadidi. Nada's face becomes mine. Nada's face becomes the girl who watches from above in the hospital corridor. I explain, I talk, I conclude. Someone is clapping. I look at Mazen, whose head is bent. There is the heavy rain of applause.

Nada seems alone now on the final slide.

Zaid and I spend the rest of the day listening, commenting, exchanging business cards, filling petitions, getting petitions filled, handing out brochures, receiving brochures, talking to funding agencies, avoiding other funding agencies. That evening Zaid and I agree to go for dinner together, "to celebrate," he says. He collects me from my room, handing me a bundle of heavy-headed tulips. He looks different. It is the suit.

"Haute Couture?" I ask,

"But of course."

We walk to the restaurant together in silence.

Vanilla

Jessica Wells

The details were vague as to why Sharon was having sex with this man. He was tall, and fairly good-looking, but that was about it. What had he said at the bar? "Hey there." And later, "You're really hot. Are you single?" She had laughed at the time because her threshold was so low that evening that, although he didn't know it at the time, he was already in her pants. She was bored and lonely and he was male, straight, and looked like he had a box of condoms at home.

He continued talking to her, but it was quite unnecessary.

His apartment was large, haphazardly decorated, and smelled oddly of baking. Sharon breathed in the sweet smell as he pushed in and out of her. She absentmindedly took his left hand and placed it on her breast. She wondered, was it cookies? Cake? Had he baked it himself, or did he have a girlfriend? She licked her lips, thinking of cupcakes, and he took it as a sign and inelegantly came, softly resting his head on her chest. She thought of pound cake, icing, and pitzelles. Her stomach growled as it often did after sex. She rubbed his back, and then slid out of bed. As he lay there dabbing his going-limp penis with a kleenex, she padded around the kitchen and found a scented candle ("Vanilla Homestyle Bakery") that he must have lit while getting the beers.

She was touched, and went back to him in bed.

Tommy the Voice

Paul Bassett Davies

Outside, the streets of Clapham were cold, dark and wet but the minicab office blazed in a fluorescent Saharan noon, battering the retina and throwing every flap of peeling wallpaper into pitiless relief. It was two in the morning and I'd been at the counter for fifteen minutes, waiting for the car that the controller had promised me in five. I didn't feel like sitting on the bench by the window: almost all of its cracked, red upholstery was occupied by a very drunk kid with bad skin and a funny haircut. He was interfering with a wrapper of fish and chips, occasionally jabbing a crab-like hand into the soggy pouch and raising a clump of food to his mouth. He dropped most of it on the way, but some of it made it in there, where some of it stayed and some fell out again, cascading down the front of his shirt and onto the floor, or the bench, or back into the wrapper. It was a bit like watching one of those cruel amusement arcade games in which a mechanical claw grabs a prize but drops it before it reaches the chute.

Behind the sliding glass partition the controller leaned into his microphone. "Seven-four, seven-four ... come in, seventy-four ... speak to me, Derek."

A squawk of static-riddled jabber erupted from a tinny loudspeaker. It seemed to satisfy the controller. "Lovely, seven-four, tell me when you're clear." From somewhere in the back came the percussive burp of an expertly-played video game. The controller's telephone rang. He picked up the receiver and adopted a tone of courtesy so insincere it amounted to mockery.

"Hello, car service ... ah, yes, sir, Mr Draycott ... Drayton, yes, you're waiting for your car from Hammersmith ... yes, we're running a few minutes late on that ... that long, is it? Sorry about that, sir ... all right, there's no need for that attitude, mate ... no, because I've just spoken to the driver this minute and he's approaching you now. The problem was, he couldn't find you because you're in the crack ... the crack between the pages of the A to Z ..." The controller looked up at me and winked. I don't know why he thought I was on his side rather than the customer's. Maybe he thought my complicity would invalidate any complaints I might have as a customer myself. Or maybe he could tell I'd had a couple of drinks. Although I was nowhere near as drunk as the kid on the bench.

"No, not in yours, no," he continued into the phone, "we use a special edition in the trade ... yes, he'll only be a minute or so now ... yes, that's number three, Archer Road, got that ... all right, sorry for the delay, sir ... yes, he's just at the end of your road now ... thank you."

The controller replaced the receiver and leaned into his microphone again. "All cars, all cars, any one Hammersmith area? We got a screamer in Hammersmith. Any one Hammersmith ...? Any one Hammersmith or Shepherd's Bush ...? Any one west of the Park ...? Any one west London...? Any one London, for fuck's sake? Come on, speak to me you tossers!"

There was another sudden burst of incomprehensible crackling from the speaker. The controller raised his eyes theatrically and responded.

"Hello, one-five, I thought you was dead. Got a job for you."

More noise from the speaker.

"No, forget your King's Cross regular, I've give that to the ayatollah. Get yer arse over to ... hang on ... three, Ashley ... no, Asquith ... can't read it ... Askey Road, Hammersmith. How long do you reckon, five minutes?"

I caught the words "bleedin' nightmare" in the crackling reply.

"Yeah, you'll do it in fifteen, easy. I'll tell him you're outside."

The controller looked up at me thoughtfully, as if trying to place me. "Oh, right, you want your car for Kentish Town, don't you?" He turned and bellowed over his shoulder, "Lenny!"

Immediately, the video game stopped and a wiry little balding guy in a torn leather jacket sidled down the narrow passage at the side of the office.

"All right, pal," he muttered as he passed me, "it's the blue Datsun."

I got in the front passenger door and sat beside him. I wanted to say something about him being there in the back room all the time I was waiting, but I didn't think I could get the right tone.

"Alright?" I said, finally, to fill the silence as he heaved at the wheel to edge from a tight parking space.

"All right for some, mate," said Lenny, managing to imply that I'd offended him, "but I tell you, this minicab driving is a game, really."

"Oh, yeah, tell me about it," I said, tuning my accent down so it was a bit closer to his own Cockney, "I've been in this game myself. Years ago." It was true but I'd only done it for about three months, and although that was plenty of time to experience the unpleasant aspects of the job, I wasn't exactly Travis Bickle. I wondered vaguely why I was trying to ingratiate myself. He was just one of those people who make you want their approval, I suppose. He didn't say anything. I was embarrassed now, and, just for something to say, I continued, "But I always reckoned it was the controllers who've got the hardest job."

He accelerated smoothly through an orange light at Queenstown Road and glanced at me thoughtfully. "What do you do now, then?" he asked.

"I make most of my living as a writer." I tried to make it sound like something only just inside the law.

"Oh yeah, a writer." Instead of asking me anything, he chewed his lip, made a controlled skid around the Vauxhall approach and swung out to pass a black Capri, the old JPS promotional model with gold lettering, once a flashy emblem of proletarian virility, now the badge of a loser so clueless he probably thought it was still cool, no irony. When the driver – a middle-aged guy with a mullet – realised he was being overtaken, he made a half-hearted attempt to speed up and aggravate us but he was too late. Lenny glanced into his rear-view mirror. "Wanker," he muttered affectionately, then he seemed to come to decision. "You were a driver, yeah?"

"That's right," I said, "just for a while, it was back in – "

"Did you ever hear of Tommy the Voice, then?"

"I don't think so. I was a driver in Bristol, actually."

"Oh, well, there you go." He made it sound as if I'd admitted to a pitiful deficiency concerning my manhood. "As it happens," he continued charitably, "Tommy the Voice was the best controller in the business. He was the Guv'nor, Tommy was. It's a gift, basically. I mean, you've been a driver, you know what it's like with some of them: leave you hanging about on the end of your rig, never get you the jobs, but Tommy was magic. Because it does take a certain type. It's like a general deploying his troops. You got to know where all your drivers are, how long before they drop off, how long they're going to take to get to the next job, taking into account the traffic, time of day, weather conditions, everything. It's like one of those Russian geezers playing chess with twenty different people at the same time." He took an unfamiliar turn after going over Vauxhall Bridge but seemed confident enough, heading through Pimlico in the right general direction.

"Never mind all these black-cab drivers with the Knowledge and all that bollocks," he said. "I mean, I respect all that but Tommy knew more about London traffic than any man alive. It's like he could sense things. He was like a crafty old spider in the middle of his web, picking up on every little tremble. A driver calls in: snarl-up on the Edgware Road. So Tommy sends the car that's just dropped off in Kilburn down to a job at Euston, going via Regent's Park to miss the jam and re-directs the one that's approaching Marble Arch from the Notting Hill end to go and pick up an account job due for half an hour in Battersea. Forward planning. Strategy. Tactics. Ever heard of Orde Wingate? He was your man: if you want creative strategic thinking applied with tactical flair, you study the Burma campaign, mate. Where was I? Oh, yeah. Another thing: Tommy didn't do drugs, like some of these controllers, speed freaks a lot of them; not that I've got anything against it necessarily, just that Tommy didn't need it."

I realised where we were when we sailed around Hyde Park corner and he pointed the nose of the car up Park Lane with the rear end swinging behind us in a lazy pendulum. "Why didn't you use Chelsea Bridge?" I asked.

"Roadworks. Anyway, Tommy the Voice was just one of those people you want to listen to. Like, some people are good with animals, Tommy was good with drivers. And it was all in the voice. Very relaxed, always in control. Like an airline pilot when they don't want you to worry, know what I mean? And that all goes back to this guy Chuck Yaeger, as it happens, that way of talking. Do you know that book called *The Right Stuff*?"

"About the astronauts. By Tom Wolfe."

"That's right, yeah," he said, sounding pleased, "have you read it?"

"I've seen the film."

"Oh. Anyway, Chuck Yaeger was the test pilot for the first American jets. Did they have that bit in the film?"

"Yes, he was played by Sam Shepard."

"Oh, interesting actor. Playwright, and all. But it was Yaeger that started all that casual style. You know, 'Houston, we have a problem ...' all of that. Understated, you might call it. And the astronauts picked it up from him, and from them it went to the airline pilots. You know, the way they come over all smooth and soothing on the announcements: 'Ladies and gentlemen,'" he said, doing a very passable imitation of a suave British pilot, "'we've got a little spot of turbulence up ahead ...' when what they really mean is they're flying straight into a fucking hurricane and the engines have packed up. To be honest, there's a bit of showing off going on there, isn't there? About how cool they can be. Same with the minicab controllers. But no-one could do it like Tommy the Voice, you've got to hand it to him."

"Is he still working, then?" I asked. I realised I wasn't following our route any more, and now, looking out into the night, I couldn't tell where we were. Somewhere up behind Lisson Grove, I thought, although it's not the way I would have gone.

"No, he died years ago. Ten, twelve years. Interesting story, as a matter of fact. He turned out to be his own worst enemy, didn't he, like a lot of them."

"Who, controllers?"

"No, great men, leaders and that. Achilles heel, feet of clay, know what I mean?

Look at Napoleon. Yeah, it all started to go wrong one Saturday afternoon."

"For Napoleon?"

"Tommy the Voice, you clown. No, this particular Saturday it was Tommy's birthday; no-one knew exactly how old he was but someone had found out the date. It was very quiet, summer holidays, and a lot of the regular work was off. A couple of drivers were watching the racing on the telly in the front office because there was no walk-in trade to speak of so Tommy didn't mind. One of the drivers was a bit of a hound for betting on the horses and he kept on at Tommy to have a flutter. The thing is, only a few of the older drivers knew about it, but Tommy had a serious gambling problem. By this time, he hadn't had a bet for years, but it's like alcohol or drugs, isn't it? You can kick the habit but you're always going to be an addict."

As it happened, this was something I did know quite a lot about, but I wasn't trying to impress Lenny any more, and I doubt that my experience would have impressed him anyway. It didn't even impress me any more. So I just said, "So it seems," and left it at that.

"Too right, mate. But this particular driver didn't know about Tommy's problem and when he phoned in a bet, he insisted on putting a tenner on for Tommy as a birthday present. So, what's the worst thing that could have happened?"

"The horse won." It was the easiest question in the world for me to answer.

"You got it. And that was it. Tommy was well and truly hooked again. Told this driver, Scottish bloke he was, to put the winnings on the next race. That was when a man phoned in for a car to take him and his pregnant wife to hospital. She was ten days overdue so she was booked in to have the baby induced. But, for once, Tommy's mind wasn't on the job: the TV in the minicab office was showing the runners for the next race by now, and Tommy and this driver, Angus, I think his name was, they were discussing the nags, checking the form, watching the odds: all the ritual that addicts wrap around the main event."

He stopped and shot me a glance. He knew that I knew all about it, I could tell. Maybe he'd been there himself. People like us send each other some kind of subliminal signal. But I just nodded and Lenny continued:

"It was only just before the race was about to start that Tommy remembered this hospital job. So, with his attention on the horses, he simply radioed the driver who was nearest the pick-up. Who happened to be a new driver in his first week on the job. No experience at all. Tommy sent him to pick the bloke and his wife up in Finsbury Park and when the driver asked him for the best way to Guy's Hospital, Tommy told him Highbury Corner, down to the Angel, over Old Street then down over London Bridge, said it was a doddle and left him to it. Now, you might say that nobody could have predicted what happened. But that's the whole point: Tommy could have, because normally he thought of everything. But now he was only thinking of one thing, wasn't he? And it was only when the driver called in to say he was stuck in thick traffic that Tommy realised he'd directed the guy down through Islington, which is always packed on a Saturday afternoon. So, with one eye on the race, which had just started, he told the driver to turn off and gave him a parallel route down through the City. Big mistake."

We stopped at a red light and when I recognised the deserted intersection I figured out that Lenny was weaving diagonally up through Maida Vale and St. John's wood in a kind of tacking manoeuvre. He drummed his fingers on the wheel as we waited. "Well, of course," he said, "an experienced driver might have been able to take up the slack when it all started to unravel. And maybe if Tommy had won again, on that second race, he'd have left it at that and got back on the ball. But probably not. If a gambler does well, he keeps betting because he's on a winning streak; and if he loses, he keeps betting because it stands to reason that his luck's about to change. But either way ..."

He accelerated away a nanosecond before the lights changed, and left a pause for me to complete the sentence for him:

"He always keeps betting," I said.

Lenny nodded gravely. "Next thing," he continued, "the driver calls in to say he's stuck in a jam on Canonbury Road. Tommy remembers there's roadworks on the new one-way system all the way down to Shoreditch. Been there for weeks. Should have remembered before. Then the driver says the woman in the back has started bleeding, she's in pain, he thinks she's going to need a doctor. Tommy tells him not to panic and he'll work something out. But even then, it didn't really get his attention. The last race was about to start and he still hadn't picked a horse. Once he'd done that, he gave the driver instructions to get him out of trouble. Or so he thought, but he wasn't thinking straight. So he didn't realise that what he'd done by now, in effect, was to direct the driver around three sides of a square, so that now the car was trying to cross the same traffic jam it had been stuck in to begin with. Then things got really bad."

Lenny paused for a moment. I had a strange urge to take over the story myself and steer it towards a happier outcome than the one I could see unfolding inside it like a malignant growth. Lenny took a deep breath and continued:

"The young driver says he's completely gridlocked now. He can't turn, he can't move, he can't do anything. And then he starts yelling down the rig, going spare. Says there's blood everywhere, he thinks she's having the baby. Tommy tries to think. He's back on the case now, but it's too late. What can he do? Call an ambulance? No, it wouldn't get through. He thinks some more. Reckons the only thing is to locate a medic somehow, and get him on a courier service motorbike. So he gets the drivers in the office to work on that, and meanwhile he puts a call out to all his drivers on the road, and other firms as well, anyone he can raise, and asks if someone can patch straight through to the gridlocked car with some emergency medical advice. But by now, the woman's gone into labour and she's haemorrhaging badly."

We reached the big intersection at Swiss Cottage and I thought it would be obvious which way to go now but Lenny turned left off Adelaide Road, and began driving through dark, leafy streets of big, expensive houses and I was lost again. When he spoke again, his voice had perked up and I thought maybe the story wasn't going to end so badly after all.

"Then a doctor did get to the car – a passing pedestrian, as it happens. He went to work like a demon to try and deliver the baby. And all the time the radio channel's open, and the young driver's giving Tommy a running commentary and Tommy can hear everything that's going on in the background, the woman screaming and the husband freaking out, and he can't do a thing, he just has to sit there in the office and listen. Finally, Tommy hears the cry of a new-born baby. The driver breaks down in tears and you can hear a bit of cheering in the background. But then it all goes quiet. Tommy keeps asking what's happening. The driver won't tell him, or can't bring himself to. Eventually he gets it out of him: the baby's still alright but the mother has died."

We crossed Haverstock Hill just above Chalk Farm and I knew where we were again now. It was the home stretch.

"That was the beginning of the end for Tommy the Voice. Once it had sunk in, he blamed himself for everything, of course. He carried on working but people said he'd lost his touch. He started working shorter hours and only did day shifts. And his voice changed. Didn't have the same ring to it, it was thinner, a bit hesitant. The confidence was gone, I suppose. And then, exactly a year later, Tommy was working a Saturday afternoon. It was very busy, there were a couple of big football games on and part of the Northern Line was shut down as well. But Tommy wasn't really on top of it. Then he starts to get a bit distant, almost a bit dreamy. Starts asking who's heading west, is anyone on the Westway, anyone leaving town, driving into the setting sun. He gets slower and slower. And all over London, all his cars were slowing down. Because the controller keeps the whole network moving, keeps it alive. But what was happening was that Tommy's heart was giving out. They talk about arterial roadways, don't they? And all his cars out there were like little corpuscles, getting more and more sluggish, just like the blood that Tommy's heart was trying desperately to pump through his veins. He put up a terrific fight, but it couldn't last. Finally, the whole network of cars flowing through the city ground to a halt. His last message was, 'All cars, stay in position.' And that was the end of Tommy the Voice."

We sat in silence for a while. Kentish Town Road. Nearly there.

"What happened to the driver?" I asked.

"What do you mean?"

"The young driver. Did he give up the job?"

There was a long pause while Lenny stared straight ahead without replying. Finally he shook his head, "No," he said, "he kept at it." There was another long pause. Lenny cleared his throat and when he spoke again he sounded glad to move on.

"Not quite the end of the story, as it happens. One week later, Saturday afternoon, you'd have had a hard time getting a minicab in west

London. And even if you'd found one, you might have got stuck in very slow traffic. There was a cortege of minicabs over a mile long for Tommy's funeral. It was wonderful, magic. The vicar had been a driver at one time and he devised a special prayer made up of minicab patter; it was something like, 'We beseech you, the controller of all things, to send your top driver, the Lord, to pick up a very special fare on account, and when you're POB, take our friend and brother Tommy the Voice to his well-earned bonus, dropping off at thy base in heaven ...' that sort of thing. Everyone loved it."

Lenny swung across the main road to make the turn to my address. "But the funny thing was," he continued, as he glanced at the house numbers, "that his wife turned up. None of us even knew he was married. And you know what she told us? Tommy had never driven a car in his life. Never even took his test. In fact, he fucking hated cars."

He pulled up neatly right outside my house. We sat in silence for a moment then I roused myself.

"What's the damage?" I asked, fishing out my wallet.

Lenny frowned at the steering wheel as if perplexed by some novelty in the concept of payment for the ride. He pursed his lips and finally he said, quietly, "That'll be twenty-eight pounds fifty."

"Christ," I muttered, "that's a bit over the odds, isn't it?"

"Well," he said, I'm charging you a bit extra for the story. Because you'll probably use it."

"What story?" By this time I was out of the car, handing three tens through his open window and making it clear with a gesture that I didn't want change.

"That story about Tommy the Voice that I just made up. You didn't believe all that old bollocks, did you?"

I just stood there with my mouth open for a moment. Then I shook my head, expelling a snort of what would have been laughter if it hadn't been mixed with more than a touch of bitterness. "As a matter of fact," I said, "I did, yes."

"Good," he said, "and just remember, you're not the only writer who's worked as a minicab driver. Goodnight, mate."

His electric window sliced up and he spun the wheel, raising one hand from it to wave briefly without looking back at me as he executed a smooth U-turn, clearing the cars parked on the other side of the road with a millimetre to spare, and surged away, back towards the lights of Kentish Town Road. I searched in my pocket for my keys. I wondered why I was suddenly feeling lonely.

The Butterfly Slippers

Rebecca Smith

I recall wondering at the time whether it was a mistake purchasing slippers with decorative butterflies attached. As it turned out my reservations were correct. I can never find them in the apartment, they constantly fly off, and are never together. I have now had to invest in a butterfly net, and must be careful not to leave the door or windows open. I have particular problems with the left one; it seems far more adventurous than the right. I arrive home to find it fluttering around the lounge, or hanging upside down from the ceiling. It wants to go anywhere but on my foot.

One fateful Tuesday I returned to find I had accidentally left a window open. After much searching I had to resign myself to the fact that the left slipper had gone. A month has passed, and I occasionally see it flying around the area. With winter approaching I have decided to buy another pair, this time with snails on; after all one slipper is of no use to anyone. They are not as pretty, but the advantage is they are much slower. In order to find them I just follow the sticky trail, invariably I locate them stuck to the wall near my potted plants.

Opening the Door

Rebecca Bryant

He was staring at the pale skin below the stern of her hat when she turned abruptly from the door. Their eyes met in a moment more intimate than either was prepared for, and the sliver of air between them frosted with confusion. He looked away, embarrassed.

"Sorry ..." her voice stumbled. "... I forgot. We can't get in this way."

He paused to gather himself on the porch of the old Boston triple-decker with its three identical apartments stacked one upon another and then followed her fleeced and booted feet along the sidewalk, through a gate, down several steps to a lawn. His heart struck his chest and his feet thudded over a crust of old snow.

It had all happened so fast. Just minutes before they'd met on the T – their first chance encounter since the divorce. He'd imagined running into her at a U2 or Outkast concert, the museum, or one of their favorite restaurants. But, no, it had happened on the T, grimy with thousands of lost memories, not just their own. And when the train slid into the Jamaica Plain station, she'd surprised him with an invitation.

"Look," she said, eyes narrow and intense as they searched his, "there's something I've been thinking about showing you. Can you come to my studio? It's only a block away."

A grey froth of commuters had parted around them, and someone dropped a cup of coffee, causing another breech in the swarm of bodies. As he'd hesitated, glancing at a clock on the station wall, the urgency had ebbed from her eyes. There hadn't been time to think. He'd simply, impulsively struck out after it, blurting, "Yes, I'd like that."

The faux fur trim of Hannah's powder blue coat wagged from side to side as she climbed the back stairs. He followed a few steps behind, noticing small dark tufts pointed with moisture. Like bristles on her favorite fitch brush. Nostalgia washed over him. He'd loved to watch her paint in the room on the east side of the brownstone, her studio until the divorce. Pictured her there late at night in jeans and a t-shirt. Heard music spilling from the stereo.

She paused, breathing uneasily. "I hope Ashaki remembered to leave the keys."

"Ashaki?" he asked absently, thoughts still at the brownstone. Something about the picture was bothering him.

"The woman I rent my studio from."

At the first landing, she tipped a brick and used a key underneath to open the rear door. Once inside, she kicked off her boots. He was still unlacing his shoes when he heard her exclaim, "Oh, no!"

He strode into a dining room. "What's wrong?"

Standing at the entrance of a hallway, she pointed. "Jackson," she said. "He's blocking the way."

He leaned into the dimly lit passage and saw a shaggy something. A large dog, its rump squashed against a door.

She said, "He tried to bite me once. See." She fingered a rip in her coat. "It left a bruise."

He swallowed hard. "Isn't there another way?"

"I wish there were, but someone broke in last week, so Ashaki changed all the locks." Her eyes darted toward the dog. "We'll have to move him."

A hard hot emotion lurched against his chest. *Time to bail,* he thought. Another voice countered: *You can't. Not now.*

"Would you mind?" she asked.

Somehow, he managed to buckle his fear and crouch just inside the hallway. "Come here, Jackson," he said. "Come here, boy." The light was bad, and there wasn't an overhead to flick on. He couldn't see the dog's eyes. *Run*, said a desperate voice in his mind. *Run.*

Just then Hannah waved a carrot-colored item shaped like a T-bone in front of him. "This is all I could find," she said.

He turned the object in his hands. "Do you suppose it's edible?"

"Well. It has all a doggie's daily nutrients."

Malcolm tapped the object against the floor. “Here you go, boy.” His tone sounded alien, even to him, and when Hannah regarded him with a look of concern, he tried to bring more authority to his voice. Still, the dog didn’t respond.

Dragging forward a chair from the dining table, Hannah said, “I’m sorry, Malcolm. I had no idea.”

“It’s all right. I’m glad to help. More than glad. You know how much ...” He wanted to say “I love you,” but instead appended “I like your work.”

“Thanks,” she said.

Her voice sounded distant: detached or preoccupied. He wasn’t sure which.

“So how are you?” she asked. “I haven’t seen you since ...” Thinking, her eyes tipped up.

“October. Five days after the divorce.” He adjusted his belt and stepped from the hall, remembering the morning the brownstone had sold. For nearly an hour, he’d parked at the curb, sorting through his Rolodex of memories, before showing up at the title company. And then it came to him. What he couldn’t remember before: he hadn’t actually seen Hannah at work for a long while.

Hannah, Hannah, Hannah. His eyes traced like kisses over her hair, shorter than he’d ever seen it, and continued over her strong brow, nose, and mouth. Then he noticed her foot, bouncing on the floor, waiting for an answer.

How was he? Lousy. But that was to be expected, wasn’t it? After six years of marriage. Finally he said, “Not too bad,” then changed the subject. “What about you? Like your new condo?”

“Beats renting,” she replied, “but change is hard.”

“Uproar’s the only music,” he murmured.

“Huh?”

“It’s Keats, more or less.” He knew she’d want an explanation, so he added, “I’ve been reading poetry; it’s helping me understand some things.”

Her eyes widened, and her mouth started to work around words but stopped. Standing, she circled the chair. “What am I going to do?” she asked the ceiling.

He didn't know what she meant and wasn't sure he wanted to. His eyes moved precisely, as if evaluating the décor, a fusion of International Style and Danish Modern, but his thoughts rambled. He wondered whether she still wore pushup bras on Sundays, a habit she'd adopted in high school when forced to attend temple. And had he missed any of Hannah's "artscapades"? Hannah's mother, Didi, had told him the story on his first pilgrimage to the altar of family scrutiny. Hannah had been seven, with a bad case of the chicken pox. Hoping to distract her from the itchy lesions, Didi brought home a set of oil paints. Hours later, with the family gathered in the kitchen for dinner, the girl had pirouetted into the room. Naked. She'd painted bright, intricate designs around every bulla within reach.

Hannah was staring out the window, toying with a ring that had replaced her marriage band. He started to ask what she was thinking, but she turned to him first. "Have any deals going, bud?"

That hurt, even though she hadn't meant it to, because it was the same question she'd asked a thousand times when he crawled home later than any decent husband would have. And now he saw what he hadn't before: instead of working all those nights, she'd been waiting for him, usually with something edible on hand. He didn't like that scenario; it was wrong, all wrong. He'd meant to be a liberated male. Instead, he'd become one of those monomaniacal corporate guys.

Without enthusiasm, Malcolm dished out the rote reply: "Baby, you know I am the king of deals." And he was. On Friday he'd beat out the big guys again, finagling a contract on a warehouse in South Boston. Eighteen months from now he'd be leasing offices on the street and condos above. Wheeling and dealing was the game he excelled at, but it didn't have the same juice any more.

Malcolm shook his watch down to his wrist and checked the time. Half past ten. Reluctantly, he slapped his leg and whistled. "What about a walk, Jackson? Let's go, boy."

An answering woof, deep and tremulous, rose from the hallway.

"He's unpredictable," Hannah said, scooting her chair back. "Be careful."

But Malcolm stepped forward, prodded by a confusing set of needs: to do something for Hannah, to hide his fear, and to see whatever it was she wanted him to see.

Snarling, the dog heaved upright. One side of his mouth lifted, revealing an incisor. Malcolm froze, eyes on the quivering snout. He knew Hannah was saying something and finally the words arranged into discernable units: “Be careful, Malc. Please. Be careful.” It was her tone that got through. He mattered to her. Still.

Malcolm backed from the hallway and shut the door. Suddenly, he was tired of the artifice. He slumped into a chair at the dining table, and after a few moments, told Hannah the story he’d never told anyone: the teeth tearing at his chubby toddler’s leg, the sound of his mother’s shovel hitting the Chow, the hospital and stitches and terror of dogs for years to come. As he talked, something loosened inside, and he wondered why he’d kept the secret so long. Telling it didn’t seem like such a big deal.

“But those scars. You said you went through a sliding glass door.”

“I’m sorry,” he said.

“Sorry?” She looked befuddled.

“I lied, Hannah. I’m sorry.”

“You said you didn’t like dogs.” Her voice broke like his had. “Why couldn’t you tell me the rest?”

The sliding glass door story was a habit, he explained. It went way back. Early on, he’d peed in his pants when anyone mentioned the dog incident. That’d been almost as bad as the attack itself, so he’d invented another explanation. (A cousin had shoved him headlong through a glass door while playing indoors.)

Her head moved back and forth in wonder.

Malcolm didn’t know what else to say. He wasn’t a liar by nature. No, he couldn’t think of anything else he’d systematically lied about. But there were patches of obscuration and avoidance, plenty of them. They hid things he didn’t want others to know. Things he didn’t like about himself.

“We’ll have to find another way into the studio,” he said.

“What’s the point?”

“I thought … ”

Hannah’s eyes slid across the floor and up to his. “Sometimes I don’t know what it’s all about. Years and years devoted to art … to marriage, even. Does any of it really matter?"

Not long ago he might have launched into a discourse about life as a cherry tree ripe with meaning. Now he knew that was just another way to avoid what he didn't want to feel, which happened to be what their divorce had forced him to feel: hopeless and disillusioned.

"Sometimes I wonder, too," he said.

"You do?" Her voice slanted with astonishment.

He nodded. She didn't say anything. Just looked at him. After a while, Malcolm scratched the ridge behind his ear. "By the way, where *is* your studio?"

She pointed to a wall decorated with masks. "There, on the other side of Mexico." Suddenly a door slammed.

He startled. "What's that?"

"It's a who, I think, not a what. Peter, the upstairs tenant."

"Couldn't he open the front door?"

"Could he? Yes. Would he? Doubtful."

She explained that she'd met Peter only once. He'd been wrangling an oversized envelope from his mailbox in the foyer when she arrived. It was summer and his torso, barely clothed in a leather vest, had bristled with hair, muscle, and tattoos. One of the tattoos was a hook. She'd started to ask if he needed help landing his catch, but he cut her off at the first consonant. "'Don't even think about talking to me, lady. I don't like dames.'"

When Malcolm shook his head with an appropriate expression of incredulity, she added: "He sounded like a twenties gangster. For all I know, he could be Mafia." In short, Hannah wasn't about to climb the next flight of stairs to borrow a key.

Malcolm stepped out the rear door. Though it was approaching midday, the overstory of May clouds had not parted. He buttoned his coat and reached for a knit cap in his pocket, pulling it over his ears. Ascending the steps, he thought, *Your mission, should you be so stupid as to accept it, is to fetch a key from an ogre."*

A brawny guy in jeans and a thin leather jacket answered his tentative knock. "Whadya want?" he asked.

“Hi, I’m Malcolm.” His hand shot forth in the businessman’s salute, but Peter ignored it.

“Whadya want?” He repeated, crossing his arms.

Malcolm’s mind skittered over several possible answers. One of them, the guy would buy. But which one?

“Look,” Peter finally said, “You’re running up my heating bill. What do you want?”

Malcolm had asked himself the same question many times since the divorce and was still clueless. Nothing had ever mattered to him as much as … A pleasant thrill ran through him. “Hannah,” he answered with all the earnestness he felt in his heart. “I want Hannah.”

“The painter downstairs?”

Malcolm nodded.

Peter cocked his head with unexpected primness. “I don’t know what this has to do with me, but go on.”

Malcolm’s eyes bounded from the door Peter had closed behind him to an aluminum chair tilted against a wall to an overturned pot with its withered stalk reaching into a void beyond the landing.

“Hannah,” Peter urged.

Suddenly Malcolm realized he was caught in an unfamiliar game – maybe not a game at all – definitely not a game. Or was it? He fumbled for words. “Okay. You know Hannah. She’s an artist. Rents studio space from Ashaki.”

Peter nodded.

“You probably don’t know much else.”

Peter shook his head.

“Well, here’s the salient point. She was married. To me.” He thought for a moment (how much did he have to tell this guy anyway?) before adding, “We met years ago.” Remembering, Malcolm smiled. He’d been working for a real estate management firm at the time. One night, leaving the office, he’d heard music and voices spill from a nearby art gallery. Briefcase in hand, he’d pressed into the crowd, moving from one cube-like room to another, until he saw Hannah, conspicuous in her quiet focus, not on the people or the party, but on the featured drawings. Positioning himself nearby, he’d asked if she was an art student, and when she nodded, had leaned over to sniff, reporting, "You can't be. You smell too good." She'd turned then, eyes fierce. "Well, I am. So check out your nose or your stereotypes."

Peter cleared his throat.

"We dated. Got married. I started a business." Malcolm was flustered. What else could he say? The guy was a complete stranger. He couldn't say the obvious, or could he?

"Okay, let me put it to you straight: I was so busy getting my business on track I derailed my marriage."

Initially she hadn't said anything at all. Next she'd joked about the situation. Then she'd asked: Couldn't he take off an occasional weekend? Leave the office a little earlier? Finally, toward what later proved to be the end of their marriage, she'd developed a fixation on getting away – far away – to Bali. "Just the two of us, together."

He'd thought there'd be plenty of time for that later. Obviously he'd been wrong. Wrong in a way that made him question his ability to get things right. And yet he still couldn't believe she'd left him; in some elemental way, it didn't make sense.

Malcolm's chest tightened with renewed urgency. "Look, can we borrow your front door key? Hannah doesn't have the new key yet and we need to get into the studio. She wants to show me something. It's important. I don't know why, but it is."

"Oh!" Peter sighed. "Is that all?"

He unhooked a karabiner from his belt and released a silver key.

Holding it out, he said, "Open the door, man. Open the door."

Five minutes later, Malcolm and Hannah stepped through the front door. Three feet across the foyer was another door.

"Now where's *my* key chain?" Hannah was rummaging through her pockets. Several coins and a lens cap fell to the ground before she found it. Malcolm followed her into the studio. It was smaller than the old one, not more than fifteen by twenty, but familiar. Pinned on a wall was an assemblage of quotes.

"This one by Montaigne is new," he said.

"You noticed."

"I notice a few things."

For a week or two, before Hannah had moved her things, he'd spent every evening in her studio, usually sipping whiskey and always wondering how he'd failed to see her growing disaffection. He'd looked for answers in the ingredients listed on the tubes of oil – cadmium yellow, viridian, Mars black; in the framed and stacked images awaiting delivery to her gallery; and especially in the quotes tidily arranged on a wall.

Hannah hooked her coat on a rack, before turning, eyes intent.

"Like what?" she asked.

"You look skinny. Someone needs to take you to Johnny's."

The intensity eased from her eyes. "I haven't been there since ..."

He looked at her. "Me neither."

Moments spilled into the room. Not illuminating like light, but building like particles of sand into a pile. The weight was more than he could handle. Malcolm turned back to the quotes.

"The great and glorious masterpiece of man is how to live with a purpose," he read. Straightening the scrap of paper, he asked: "Is that what you're looking for?"

"That's the point, isn't it?"

He liked the way her eyes filled when she smiled.

"Problem is," she continued, "I'm stuck on the antecedent. Is there a purpose – a single purpose?"

Moving toward a stack of canvases, Hannah glanced at him, realized he was waiting for an answer, and said, "I don't think so."

She was flipping through the canvases. He waited until she pulled one out and placed it in front of the others before moving closer. Two yellow cubes tilted against rectangular shadows on a background of burnt sienna. The cubes were banded with horizontal white lines where she'd scratched down to the canvas. He bent forward. There was something vulnerable about the painting. He couldn't say what.

"It doesn't makes sense," she continued, "not with everything we know about the universe. I mean, does a star have a purpose? Does gravity? Maybe we're here like everything else – a chance manifestation of the cosmos."

"Would that be so terrible?" he asked.

She shrugged. “Depends on what else you’ve got going on.”

That was Hannah, the tough girl. It reminded him of another artscapade. In the fifth grade, Hannah had informed her parents that she’d had enough of art books. To be an artist, it was essential to see the real stuff, which was, of course, in New York City. When could they go? Her parents’ amused response had not been at all satisfactory, so Hannah, who knew a thing or two about good citizenship from her father, a history teacher, had launched a petition drive. Friends, neighbors, even the plumber – all had been fair game. The names had added up quickly and the pressure, too, Didi had explained on Malcolm’s next trip to Cleveland. She’d opened a scrapbook, pointing to ruled sheets of paper with two hundred and forty-seven signatures. Taped to the opposite page were ticket stubs from the Met, Moma, Whitney, and other museums.

“What do you think?” Hannah interrupted his thoughts.

It took him a minute to remember the topic. “I think the universe has a maker of some sort, and where there’s a maker, there’s a purpose.”

“What if your maker is a particle of superheated matter?”

“Some like it hot.”

She frowned, so he said, “Give me a break, Han. I’ve read a book or two.”

“Okay, so what do you *really* think?”

He shrugged. “I think of God as an intelligent force, not directing the cosmos, but unifying it into patterns.” He nodded toward the painting. “Like that.”

She ran a hand over the image. “Making something from nothing …”

“Sort of.”

“A cosmic creative force.”

“I guess. Sure,” he said.

Her fingers tapped against the drafting table. “Does believing in a maker give you a sense of purpose?” she asked finally.

Malcolm placed his black leather shoe on a chair and propped his arms across his knee, thinking. “Well, it makes things fit together. It helps me feel related to everything else.”

“That doesn’t sound like purpose,” she said. “It sounds like a sense of place … of belonging – here on this Earth, in the Milky Way, in the cosmos."

"Here in this room," he said, eyes softening, "with you."

She looked away. After a while, she said, "Art used to give me that."

"Used to?" He looked around the room; it did have a dusty, unused feeling.

"Things change," she said.

"Yeah, I've noticed that too ..." And then an idea occurred to him: "I think you have to be open to change, or maybe just open. That's when I feel connected."

Hannah nodded, as if pleased. After a bit, she riffled through the canvases and brought another to the fore – white lines and specks gouged from an indigo background. Looking at it gave him a strange feeling.

"Is this what you wanted me to see?" he asked. "Your new work."

"No."

"So why am I here?"

She closed her eyes and took a deep breath.

"Well?"

You won't like what I'm going to show you."

"Show me."

Hannah threw her shoulders back, and in a burst of activity that confused him because at first he thought it meant something else, she moved away from the window, pulled a sweater over her head followed by a turtleneck, and tugged on the straps of her bra. He was too startled by what he saw next to react to the fact that she was wearing a pushup bra. There were raw red marks on her chest where her right breast had been. A dozen responses exploded in his brain but he held them back and let himself feel instead and then he started to cry and she did too. When he opened his arms, she stepped forward. Her body was different against his now; feeling this, he gripped her tighter. They took harbor in each other in a way he couldn't remember ever having done before, like two ships nosed up to the same dock. Finally, he asked the question he didn't want to ask: "Did you know about this before the divorce?"

She brushed her eyes against his shirt, nodding. "I wasn't sure you could handle it, Malc. I wasn't sure you'd show up for me. I couldn't take the risk. It would have been too awful."

That she'd had the strength to leave, when most people would have grabbed onto just about anything, astonished him. He felt ashamed too. What a wall he must have been. But as he stared at the scar, wondering what else might be sealed inside her, it occurred to him that he, Hannah – everyone, for that matter – hid things out of fear that they wouldn't be able to manage certain difficult feelings. He took a deep breath and let it out, looking squarely at her chest. The surgeon had attempted to disguise the cuts by placing them in the contour of her body but the marks were deep.

"Can I touch?"

She nodded.

He traced the lines with a finger. "It's abstract, like your art, but I think I see something in it."

"What's that?"

"A vacation in Bali?"

She pulled away.

"A weekend on the Cape?"

Hannah reached for her clothes.

"All right then," Malcolm said, smiling. "How about lunch at Johnny's?"

She lifted her coat from the rack. "You've got yourself another deal, bud."

God's Fingerprint

Rob Pateman

I haven't seen her for twenty odd years but I recognise Mandy instantly. It's the dimple in her chin that gives her away. Her hair is darker, her face fuller but her eyes are still as brown and flat as puddles. And the dent in her jaw is as deep as it always was. Deep enough to fit my forefinger snugly.

Seeing her stare from the television screen slaps me. The news reader's face is stern, his voice low and slow. A train crash. Seventy dead. A car on the line at a crossing. Mandy's car. The reporter at the scene says police are speculating why she was there.

'Because God didn't want her,' I say.

He never had. That's what I'd told her when she was about six and me eight. She was on her way home from the sweet shop. I was bored.

The damage we can do in a moment.

'See that,' I'd said, sticking my finger into the dimple in her chin. 'That's where God took one look at your face and pushed it away with his finger.' Her head snaps to the left from the force of my finger. Click.

She hardly ever came outside again. A year later I moved. The last time I saw her she was sitting at her living room window. I wagged my finger at her. She put her hand over her chin and began rocking herself slowly, as if I'd set a metronome going.

Tick-a-tick-a time bomb.

A Life

Barry Troy

When Mam ran away to Fuertaventura with our neighbour Mrs. Cuddihy the sky fell in.

Frankie Cuddihy stormed in to see my father. He was savage – no holding him. Brutal he was, beat the bejaysus out of Da, and Da's no joke as a scrapper. It was uncalled for – anyone'd think it was Da who'd run off with his wife. What could Da do about it? But then, Frankie Cuddihy was never long on brains. Mam used to say he was thick as a ditch after rain.

He wouldn't have beaten Da under normal circumstances. Da was asleep on the chair and it was twelve o'clock of a Friday night. Da was langers – he's always langers by that time Friday night. Frankie Cuddihy took advantage of him. I knew by the look of Da when I read out Mam's farewell letter to him that the message wasn't getting through, wasn't registering. As a result, when Frankie woke him with a belt in the mouth he hadn't a clue what was going on. Frankie was able to get three more good ones in before Da got up out of the chair. Frankie had the advantage from the word go so, like I say, there was no call for him to roar and shout and fill the neighbours' mouths with gossip.

I had turned sixteen at the time. Mam relied on me to look after things. She said she could feel her destiny welling up inside her. Mam was always saying things like that. She used to get up at all hours of the night and watch the Open University on television. Gay sex always interested her too. She told me before she left – the afternoon I helped her pack – that she had found her true personality. Standing at the window, holding a folded cardigan to her chest, she said I would realise what she meant when I was older. Mam had no notion that me and Billy Cuddihy had been doing it for nearly three years at that time or that we'd tried three-in-a-bed months before. Mam was still living in old-God's time, but I didn't blame her for that.

What annoyed me – really pissed me off – was all her talk about women's lib. When all's said and done, it's one thing to shag off and do your own thing – men have been doing that for years – but another thing altogether to do the dirty on a sister, in this case me, her sixteen-year-old daughter, if you see what I mean. Germaine Greer, how are you!

If she was going to do her own thing she could have taken at least a few of the smaller ones with her, not left me to bring up the eight of them on my own. She knew bloody well that Da was going to be more of a hindrance than a help.

For months after she left Da needed more attention than the baby. He went into shock and then straight into denial. Least that's where Margaret Connolly from the Social said he went. Great bloody place to be, I can tell you. He denied every damn thing. He was great at it, a first class denier. Nothing was his fault, and too much time – time I could ill-afford to waste – was spent humouring him, listening to his whinging. I can tell you it wasn't easy having your mother in Fuertaventura and your father in denial and you tripping over eight children.

Mam was a great one for demanding her space. She was always shouting that a person needed space for this and space for that. Divil a bit of space she left me for watching the Open University I can tell you.

Apart from the odd afternoon roaring at Oprah Winfrey, Billy Cuddihy was my only relaxation, my little bit of space. Gone were the carefree days we spent in the park shaggin' our dakes out and drinking cider. Now we had to be sneaky about it. After the punch-up, Da couldn't abide any member of that family near the house. Billy and I had to manage standing up in the garden shed a lot of the time. Only when Da was pissed could we use the bed; even then the two little ones would blackmail me, threaten to tell, or pee all over us at the right wrong moment, if you know what I mean. It wasn't that the kids understood what we were doing in the bed we had to share with them – after Mam left they wouldn't sleep on their own. The power they had over me was the fact that they realised Da would go nuclear if he knew a Cuddihy was sleeping under his roof and him only across the landing.

It was total. Mam just walked out of our lives. She had always been full of sayings, always had buckets of quotations to justify what she wanted to do. Clever bits and pieces she'd heard on television or read in the books she was always stuck in. "Gone from our gaze like a shit in a river" was one of them. That's what she did to me.

The little ones hadn't a clue what was going on. They were so used to expecting me to do everything that I don't think they noticed for three months or so that Mam was gone. Kathleen, the next one down from me, was nearly fifteen and she was the most difficult. I had to slap some sense into her to bring her around. Looking back on it, I suppose it affected her more than the others. She was always sensitive. Mam had a soft spot for sensitive people, said they needed to be gentled along. That's all very fine if they're your own.

Sensitive or not, Kathleen had to be made look life in the kisser, had to buckle down to reality. After all, I may have been hard on her, given her the odd clip on the ear, but in the end of the day she'd have to admit it was me that had the carving knife the time Da went queer and thought he could get his rocks off with her. That was some Friday night I can tell you, but least said soonest mended.

It was four months before we got the postcard. It was addressed to "All". The card said "Hi! Having a ball!!! Think of you every day! Love! Mam." There was a picture of this fantastic beach, the bluest sea ever invented, and this woman with the best pair I ever saw waving out at me. I sat down in the wet kitchen to study it.

It was not a good day. The electricity final-demand arrived with the card. The milkman had called earlier that morning – a decent stick – and told me there was no way he could leave anything until a down payment was made. He wouldn't even reconsider for a quickie in the hall.

The breakfast things were still on the table and the sink was full of crockery. The two little ones were crawling all over a pile of washing on the floor. The baby needed changing and was bawling away to beat the band. I looked at the card for a long while. "Hi! Having a ball!!!" I think it was those exclamation marks that did it. Something snapped in me that day.

I rushed up to their room and took Kate Millet's *Sexual Politics* out of the drawer where Mam hid it and brought it down to the kitchen. I tore out each page separately and then tore every one into four pieces and let the pieces fall to the floor. I'd never attacked a book before. It wasn't really the book I attacked – it was Mam. It was what you might call a defining moment and it felt great. I think I began casting around for a way out after that morning. I used to dream of your woman with the tits and the way she was gallivanting on that fabulous beach. Not a stitch or a care on her. She was far from denial. Just like the advertisement for the Lottery, "That Could Be You," I'd say to myself in the broken mirror over the lavatory.

A year went by. Da was walking carefully, almost tiptoeing you might say, when I was around. The night with the carving knife had sort of quietened him. Even so, 'tis hard to kill a bad thing. Friday nights were still Friday nights. Bugger all had really changed.

When he looked sideways at me that Thursday night and told me to clean the place, I knew there was something in the wind, that he was planning something. He'd never noticed before whether the place was clean or not.

"Why?" I said, and kept my head down over the button I was sewing into Thomas's shirt for school the next morning.

"Friend," he said. "I might be bringing a friend home."

"What kind of a friend?" I said.

"A friend," he said, raising his voice to stiffen it, trying to put that old don't-question-your-father tone into it. "My friends are my business."

"Then your friends can clean the place," I said, in a reasonable tone. "That's your business too."

He said nothing for a while. Then he put a tenner on the table.

"Give th'ould place a clean for us," he said.

I started another button, pretended tenners arrived every night.

"This friend," I said. "Wouldn't be a she friend by any chance, would it now?"

"That is definitely none of your business," he said, adopting the tone he used for getting everyone out to Mass on Sundays, even held up a finger.

I have to admit I was curious. I wanted to see what kind of a woman would pick up with a man that had as many children as Da. He was handsome enough, mind you. He was going on thirty-five at the time. Ma was fifteen when he put her in the family way with me. He was just over the six-foot and as strong as a bull from all the tearing and dragging he did down at the builders' suppliers where he worked. He had a bit of a beer belly but he cleaned up well. If you didn't know his circumstances you could mistake him for a great catch.

Tracy she called herself.

The two of them were well away by the time they arrived around midnight. I was out of breath and watching Richard Gere when they came in. Billy and I had done it every which way after I'd fired everyone off to bed and Billy had disappeared over the garden wall as soon as we heard Da's key in the door. I remember wondering if she'd notice my panties on the floor by the sofa.

She was about twenty-five – a bottle-blonde with a grand little arse on her. He kept feeling it as he introduced me to her. It was obvious he could hardly wait to get the leg over. Tracy had a big nose. I could see straight away the nose was why she was with him. If the girl had the money for a nose job she'd wave day-day to him in the morning. Funny that. There she was, as good a body as Julia Roberts and probably better, but that nose was holding her back. I mean men only want us for one thing and our noses have nothing to do with that. Mind you, Tracy's had possibilities – but that's just me being bitchy.

"Get us a couple of glasses, some ice and a jug of water," he said.

He knelt down at the music centre and began fiddling with it. Man never knew how to use it even when it was working. Jason had stuck a lollipop stick into it weeks before.

"Thass Richard Gere," Tracy said, trying to focus on the box, one eye closed.

"Spot on," I said, not moving, not getting glasses.

"I asked you for glasses," he said, sitting back on his heels, putting on his boss-man look for Tracy's benefit.

She looked embarrassed and that changed my mind about her. I got the glasses and water.

"What about the ice," he said, beginning to think he was in charge.

"The fridge hasn't worked for three months," I said.

I left them to it.

I was still awake when they hit the feathers. I could hear the bed creaking into the night and I thought about them and myself and wondered if Mam was creaking another bed somewhere else at that very moment.

It was then the plan came to me. I decided I would have to go to Fuertaventura and try to persuade her to come home and let me get a life. Tracy was the key. First I had to make friends with Tracy. Tracy would keep him away from Kathleen when I left. I was like the farmer with the fox and the goose and the bag of meal trying to cross the river.

Typical of a man of his limited imagination he was on top banging away when I brought them their breakfast in bed. He was so surprised I'd say he lost it. Later on, when she came down, I made her another cup of tea and I think she was glad of a bit of female company after all she'd been through. The bed had been going like a machine gun all morning.

I really sucked up to her and she fell for it all the way. As time passed she took to staying two, then three nights a week. When she started bringing croissants for their breakfast I knew I had her where I wanted her.

For six months I put away money and terrorised the kids into silence. I was ruthless. I held onto most of the Children's Allowance, kept back money that should have gone on clothes, saved on the food. Towards the end I let bills mount up more than usual.

Billy Cuddihy kept the small bag for me overnight. We had our last quickie behind their front door before he saw me to the bus stop. I arrived in Lanzarote at one o'clock that afternoon.

I sat in a bar at Playa Blanca waiting for the ferry to Fuertaventura. I'd never felt that weight of sun on my shoulders. A grand-looking Swedish lad bought me a lager. He was the first person I ever heard speak of Jandia. It fascinated me. It sounded like something out of *The Lion, the Witch and the Wardrobe*. We sailed over together and I was so light-headed and happy in myself and so warm in the sun I let him do it behind a lifeboat. Not the biggest bang ever, but the sheer idea gave me a buzz, really kick-started the holiday. I felt great going down the gangplank waving goodbye to my blond Swede, dead pleased that I hadn't a clue who he was and happy that I didn't care. It was my first thrilling experience of being anonymous.

After three days I got news of Mam from an Irish barman in Corralejo and I traipsed on down the coast trying the bars. It was Mrs. Cuddihy I met first. I found her the second day I was in Puerto del Rosario. She was doing checkout in a small supermarket and nearly dropped her drawers when she saw me. Mam worked nights in a bar and they shared this manky studio apartment – it was tiny – in the old part of town. Why they called it the old part I don't know. The whole place looked bloody old and decrepit to me. The apartment block they were in needed a coat of paint and someone to take the grass and the cockroaches out of the roof. They weren't exactly bursting their knickers with delight at my visit.

I'll be honest. Looking at the two of them, for the life of me I couldn't see what they saw in one another. Thinking back on that day and the way they avoided looking at each other, I reckon that they both had reached that conclusion as well, but didn't know what to do about it. They were like me the first time Billy Cuddihy put it in – didn't know whether to move forward or back.

Mam was surprised. Fair play to her, she managed to give me a hug in an awkward, fumbly kind of way. She really pissed me off though by asking how the kids were one after the other. Not once did she ask me how I was getting on, was I happy, was I in denial or in any other bloody thing. She assumed I had to be OK. Good old Rocky!

I told her Shane had gone into decline and was pining for her. He wasn't, but I told her that because she was weak about Shane, him having been delicate since the day he was born. I knew it was a sure thing to get her to go home. I also knew that Shane would bear me out – the minute she'd arrive he'd get weak again to grab her attention.

I realised as soon as I said it that I'd given her the excuse she'd been looking for. From that day on she worked toward going home. I said nothing about Tracy. Mam didn't ask, and I didn't say. I think Mrs. Cuddihy was just as happy they were splitting. She picked up with a Croatian who played a squeeze box in one of the pubs. I heard later he turned out to be a real bastard. You win some, you lose some.

I told Mam I had to meet a friend on the Jandia Coast – God, how I love that name – and I got a lift all the way there in a delicatessen van that smelled fantastic. I slept on the beach for a few nights. I lazed in the sun and swam naked in roaring surf, just like your woman on the card. It felt good to meet the dawn alone – no kids, no nappies, no Da, no one to look after but myself.

Fourth day in Morro Jable I was having a coke and watching this fella make a balls of cleaning the cafe I was in.

I strolled up to him with the empty can. I was wearing an obscene tee shirt, denim cut-offs and not a damn thing besides. I knew he just had to think all his Christmases had arrived.

"I'm good at that," I said. "I can clean much better than you."

He put down the cloth. He was a young guy with a nice face, great teeth and good brown eyes. He reminded me just a teenchy bit of Richard Gere.

"You cook?" he said.

"Delia Smith ain't in it," I said.

"Who Delia Smith?" he said.

He looked nice with his forehead all crinkly, his black curly hair coming forward.

"Doesn't matter," I said. "I'm a good cook. I have eight brothers and sisters."

That got his attention.

He grinned then.

"You make nice love?" he asked, Romeo-like, pushing out his lower lip, grinning saucily.

I pinched his nose.

"Like an angel," I said.

I took the cloth away from him and went behind the bar.

I had a life.

The Plan

Anthony M. O'Sullivan

Charlo held tight to Vinney's waist and struggled to keep the sawn-off shotgun concealed beneath his coat that flapped wildly in the breeze.

Vinny coasted the motorbike to the edge of the footpath. The street was empty, just as he planned. "Piece a cake," he said over his shoulder.

Charlo didn't trust himself to answer. He dismounted and walked towards the post office, legs rubbery, right knee banging against the shotgun, forcing him to take short, quick steps. Once inside, the gun was out before he saw the crowd in the office. There must have been twenty or more, all elderly, all looking at Charlo with shocked, watery eyes. He hadn't figured on this.

"A ... a robber!" came a woman's voice, shrill and high, followed quickly by a gravelly baritone full of menace: "Fuck off ya little shite. You're not getting' my pension."

Charlo froze. Oh, Christ! It's pension day! He stumbled backwards into the street, saw the motorbike, heard the tic, tic, tic of the engine, but there was no Vinney. He tried to steady himself. A siren wailed in the distance. Vinney appeared from around a white van parked across the street, licking a Mr Whippy, his eyes tiny slits of pleasure. He saw Charlo and looked surprised, "Jaysus! That was quick!"

"It was full of oul wans!"

"Course it was. There'd be no fuckin' money if it wasn't!" The sirens grew louder and garda cars entered both ends of the street.

"That was the bleedin' plan."

The Guards Came to the House

Hugo Kelly

The Guards came to the house on Thursday and said to my mother you're going to the Joy. She said all right and followed them out of the house and into the squad car. I was watching television. Sandy came home a few hours later.

"Where's Jenny?" he said.

"The Guards took her to the Joy," I said.

"The cunts," he said and kicked the chair a few times before staring out the back window for a while. I watched him, trying to work out whether he was good Sandy or bad Sandy. He lit a cigarette and swallowed the smoke. He tapped his foot on the ground. It's bad Sandy, I thought.

"You know what we should do about this," he said.

"No I don't," I said.

"We should kill a Guard," he said.

"How would we do that?" I asked.

"With a car."

"We don't have a car."

"Don't worry, I'll get a car," he said.

He was gone for about fifteen minutes. Then I heard a beep outside the door. I ran outside all excited. There was Sandy, smiling like a proud father even though the car was old and knackered with grimey seats. It belonged to Mrs. Grimes down the road. I opened the door and got in. It smelt of fart. Sandy was looking at himself in the mirror and rubbed his hand through his yellow hair preening himself like I'd often seen him do.

"Didn't have time to be fussy with the wheels," he said. "You don't have a comb do you?"

I shook my head. He grimaced and kicked the accelerator. The car almost jumped into life. Then we were skidding down the road bouncing over the speed ramps. The car creaked and groaned. The kids stopped playing and cheered. Mrs. Grimes stood in her front garden and looked at us. Her face was blank. She was an old thing with blue hair and booties and a face like a used teabag. "She never uses the fucking thing anyway," Sandy said.

"Yeah," I said. Stealing from your neighbours was something Sandy liked doing. They were always too afraid to call the Guards.

We drove onto the motorway. The clouds were smeared across the sky, thin and grey like strands of hair. Sandy began to sing. It was something he did when he was happy. He loved driving even an old banger like that one. He beat his palm on the steering wheel. There was a funny colour in his eyes like he was burning inside and the blazing light was escaping. I had never seen him so happy. Never. Not when he drank with Mam and told her that she was as good-looking as Kate Moss. Or when he saw the horses fall in the Grand National. Or when a priest got done for sex abuse. He was happier than all those things put together.

He pushed the car on faster and it was like he was doing it with the squeezed tension in his shoulders and scrawny neck. We were up behind cars, braking and skidding and skewing from side to side. They pulled over and slowed down or just acted frightened. I felt so excited. I even forgot I was afraid of Sandy. We left the motorway and we were back in the estates again. There were cars and vans and lorries and the shopping centre and the Argos and the McDonalds and the remnants of the old church and the farm. But there were no Guards. Not outside the shopping centre. Not cruising around the estates like they were tourists or something.

"Do you know why they took Mam away?" I asked Sandy.

"Because they could," said Sandy. "Because they can."

He started to hit the steering wheel again and I could see the laughter leaving him, being burnt off by the new anger pouring out of his dry lips and yellow skin. The joy was gone. This was always the way with Sandy.

"Where are the fuckers?" he screamed.

He began to weave a bit on the road and it was hard to enjoy the drive thinking at any moment we were going to end up wrapped around some pole like what happened to the Cuniffe twins. Then I saw a light ahead pulling out of a side road just as we passed. I let a roar.

"Back there a squad car."

"Where?" he said.

"Behind you."

"Where?"

"Look behind you," I said like this was all some panto.

Sandy was happy again. He began to clench his fist as if he was about to punch someone. At the first break in traffic he braked hard and swung the car around. There was fierce beeping from everywhere. Sandy accelerated again. He was swinging the car like he didn't care what happened. One by one the cars on front disappeared, diving into turnoffs and estates like frightened rabbits. He nudged us closer and closer. We were both shouting with excitement. Kill a Guard. Kill the Guard. Kill any Guard.

We were almost behind it when I realised it wasn't a squad car. Nothing but some white van with those emergency lights on top. Sandy let a bellow and pulled the car onto the pavement.

"How hard is it to find a Guard in this city," he screamed.

And then he began to laugh. Thick guffaws of plegmy laughter.

"Not to worry, Tallaght wasn't built in a fucking day," he said and giggled to himself until spit was running out his mouth and his eyes had gone kind of red, the colour of raw meat. "We're going to hunt down a Guard cos they've done us wrong. Am I right?"

"You're right," I said.

So we took off again and drove around for a while longer. I started to get hungry and Sandy went quiet like he does from time to time.

Then suddenly we were trapped by the evening traffic. It came from everywhere like a giant net. We couldn't escape it. Every road we went. Lines of cars and SUVs lined up waiting for the blinking of far-off traffic lights. Sandy started getting agitated. He pulled off down narrow short cuts, rat-running through estates. But it was no good. We were caught in a mile-long tailback like everyone else.

"Fuck this," Sandy said after a few minutes.

He swung the car halfway onto the path and drove on the inside all the way up to the lights. There was mad beeping but Sandy let out a bellow as he pulled across the road, cutting off cars in every direction. We were back on the motorway. But even there after a mile of freedom we ran into more traffic. There was nowhere for us to go. Sandy began to shake with frustration.

"What's this? What sort of city has roads like this? Jesus what sort of infrastructure have we?"

He was getting madder and madder like he did once a week, usually on a Sunday when it was hard to get a bus into town to rob.

"You can do nothing in this city. Nothing. You can't even kill a Guard. You can't even find a squad car. That's how useless it is. That's how awful it is. It's the worst place in the world."

I could see that his face was going white and his eyes seemed to lose colour disappearing in his face. I looked out. It began to rain. Heavy dirty Irish rain that makes you want to give up. The car in front moved on a couple of feet and I could see there had been some sort of an accident ahead. There were a couple of cars jammed together like a couple of dogs fucking. Then I saw there was a Guard, tall and thick like a blue tree standing not far away directing traffic around it.

"A Guard, Sandy," I whispered.

But there was no reply. Sandy's head was resting against the steering wheel. His hands still clenched the wheel, the knuckles milk white against his margarine coloured skin.

"Sandy," I said again and touched his shoulder.

But he was gone now. Whatever he had got this morning had worn off. Now he would sleep in a coma until he woke and began all over again. I could see the Guard was doing his fancy hand signals making faces at the traffic like he was constipated or something. The cars on front began to move. We stayed completely still. A car behind beeped and then another. I opened the car door and got out. I looked around and there in the grass verge was a flat stone. So I picked it up and it sat nicely in my hand. The beeping got worse and the Guard looked in our direction but like a true Guard he ignored the hassle for as long as possible. I could hear car doors opening and the sound of knocking on glass. I looked at the grey useless sky and the murky clouds. From here I could see over the estates, see the horizon blocked by the tall buildings of the city. If I paid attention I could see the chimneys of the Joy. I imagined my ma in some cell with a load of hardjaws, ugly whores with bad teeth and even worse makeup. And more junkies like Sandy except sadder and thinner and even more desperate. And that was hard to think about. But what was harder was that I knew Ma wouldn't find it so bad. At least there would be bread in a bread bin somewhere.

I stopped and opened my mouth feeling the wet linger on my face. I was angry and the anger made me hot and the cold didn't bother me. "Come here, Guard," I said to myself. And suddenly I was running with the stone and it was already fired. I could see it lobbing through the air. I could feel its energy carrying me along. And it was good for once not to feel tired or hungry or worried that Sandy might burn the house down or that my mother would ever smile again or whether there would be any bread for toast. Or if there was bread would there be any butter. Or if there was any butter whether there would be any point at all in eating it.

The Guard was walking in my direction but when he saw me running he stopped. His eyes flicked behind me, checking out the beeping before again focusing warily on my face. He moved a bit to the side, keeping out of the way, then took more steps when he saw I wasn't slowing down. Next thing he was looking scared, scrambling across the grass. But I moved like a bird and jumped at him, stone looking for its target. I heard him cry out. I think I heard someone else scream. I was on him and for a moment I saw the panic in his squinty eyes. And his tongue was sticking out of his mouth like a worm. And I brought the stone down with all the effort I had but he shifted his head, so it caught the edge of his cap, knocking it off, and then just glancing his shoulder. He let out a bellow like he'd been shot. The stone dragged me down to the ground and I cursed my bad aim. At most I'd broken his shoulder but maybe not even that. I could hear him huffing and puffing behind me. There was a funny peace like the gap between TV programmes and before the ads start. I got up and looked at him and he looked at me and he looked frightened again as he clutched his shoulder. Then he started shouting. "I'll get you" and "you're for it" and all that. But nobody came to help. All the lines of traffic were silent and I could sense the frightened faces behind the flapping windscreens. It was like the world was holding its breath. I glanced back and saw that Sandy was still asleep in the car. But nobody was hassling him now. So I decided I'd done enough and walked away. Behind me there were no sounds except for the whine of the Guard and the nervous rumble of car engines. I walked along the motorway staring at the spiky dead shrubs and the pulpy rubbish staining the ground. The rain paused and the clouds opened and a shy sun appeared and I could feel a soft warmth through my wet clothes. It gave me some energy and I walked and walked leaving the tailback of cars far behind. I knew no Guards would appear or none would stop me.

In time I came to the roundabout that led to the shopping centre. From there I left the road and headed along the muddy paths through the empty pitches. It was getting dark and the soft blue lights came on burning like matches. Soon I came to the estate. Everything was silent. For a moment I thought about telling Mrs. Grimes that her car was ok but I didn't because when I got onto our road, I saw that there were lights on in the house. Ma was home from the Joy. She was standing in the kitchen when I got in. There was a smell of cooking. She smiled at me. It was a while since I had seen her smile like that. Maybe Christmas when Sandy turned up with a turkey dinner from Marks and Spensers that he'd probably robbed.

"You're soaked," she said.

"How come you're back?" I asked.

She opened the oven and poked at the oven chips.

"Oh, it was all a mistake. They had the wrong person, wrong estate. They got it sorted in a few hours. They were very nice. I met a very nice probation officer. He helped me with the welfare."

I could see by her she'd had a good day. It had been a break.

"Where's Sandy?" she asked.

I shrugged my shoulders.

"Don't know. I was just out," I said.

"Change out of them things," she said as she lit a John Player Blue, "and we'll have a gammon steak and some chips and beans."

"Yeah," I said. "I'm famished."

Then she came over and looked me in the eye, kind of half smiling and it felt kind of half familiar. It reminded me of some time before Sandy and the others when it was just the two of us.

"You're a good lad," she said. And then she hesitated and I hesitated but she leaned forward and took my shoulders and pressed them. And as she did that I felt something fall away from me. I felt lighter, happier again. So I went upstairs and put on an old tracksuit and then I ate like a warrior. Ma hid some money so that Sandy wouldn't find it. I watched television and fell asleep on the couch. It had been a mad day.

Poor Cow

Tessa Green

She has the feeling in her stomach that means she's in love. It's the same as before her driving test. She always fails. The fourth time her aunt gives her a beta blocker. It doesn't help; her heart still pounds.

When she meets him with sandwiches and a flask, she's already thinking of how she can make a next time happen.

He drives up the A1. She thinks *she* wouldn't pass him as he goes through lights at amber and sits on someone's tail; flicking sideways to get by.

The leaves are golden. They stick like shit (he says) to their shoes. Down in the valley by the ochre stream she sniffs, 'There's something dead down there.'

'Oh, yer?'

'It's sweet and sickly.' She's proud that she can tell.

Mooching behind her, he talks of a girl he's spanked. 'Why don't you ever spank me?' she thinks.

On the slippy bridge, she has cheddar and piccalilli sandwiches and tea; he a packet of Cheesy Whotsits and a roll-up. She daren't touch him although his knee is so close it could be hers. She breathes in his exhaled smoke; gobbles up his yellow stained finger on the sly.

Because she has the right boots on, her feet aren't wet as they cross the stream and see the cow lying on its back, blown up like a balloon. And from its cunt (he says) there's a calf, half in half out.

Now he can smell it.

At the Intersection of Heaven and Hell

Susi Klare

A skinny girl wearing nothing but boots and goggles pumps toward me on her bike. I get a quick look at her nipples before she's lost in the dust. People drift in and out of sight, we're all wandering around dusted with white playa powder. Young and old alike, our hair, our beards, our moustaches are the same grey.

All these dust storms keep blowing me back to Iraq. Not that I've ever been to Iraq, but this is what I do these days, I try to imagine what it's like in that other doomed-to-hell place. It's been five months since the invasion. Five months and the devil knows how much longer. My buddy Wayne said Burning Man would take my mind off Iraq.

Yeah, right.

So we drove across the mountains and through endless miles of sagebrush. We drove all night and through half the day to get to this ephemeral city in the middle of this flat white desert. We entered the mayhem of Black Rock City, threw up a couple of tents and a canopy, and then Wayne changed into a silky red slip – not my thing, but hey, it's a free country – and he took off on his bike to view the art. And now it looks like the air has cleared enough that I can lift my goggles and try to enjoy the view of the two girls walking in front of me. Their thonged asses, how they work their walk into the beat – the techno beat that's machine-gunning from on high, from some metal tower. These girls look about the same age as my daughter, my Melissa. The short one's got an eagle tattooed across her back. Devil knows, she's stuck with it for the rest of her life.

And I'm just a dick in the dirt tourist in search of a can.

The air clears to a painful brilliance, and I can see where a distant row of porta-potties stand side by side like soldiers in the sun. Bleak mountains off in the distance, not a breath of living green, and that missing piece of horizon where a dust devil is gathering itself to blast us into the next whiteout.

I get in line behind a deeply tanned guy with a sweaty beer bottle. He's talking to a nipple-pierced girl who's cultivating a killer sunburn. He's telling her about some camp run by fishermen from Oregon, bragging how he gorged on plate after plate of free salmon and tuna. I see the guy shoveling blackened fish into his greasy mouth. I see the girl getting fried by the sun. I see her blister and peel and in twenty or so years sprout a malignant melanoma which will metastasize to her brain and kill her dead. And if she has a child by then, that poor child will have to be raised by the random scruff who seeded it.

Porta-pottie doors squeak open and slam shut. Some woman with the voice of a heavy smoker announces to the crowd that she just had the best shit ever. People cheer.

Not my thing, but hey.

I untie the orange bandana from around my neck. It's for slipping over my mouth when the dust gets bad, but I shake it out and lay it across the burnt girl's shoulders. Before she can say anything, I turn and ask the fish guy for directions to the free fish.

He shakes his head and laughs. "It doesn't matter," he says. "With greedheads like me around, they've gotta be out of fish by now." He heads into the next empty can. Another one opens up and the girl tries to give me back my bandana.

"No, please," I say, as if it weren't already too late. "It's yours," as if anything I do could make a difference.

***

Wayne and I are drinking gin and tonic. We're in lawnchairs under the scant shade of our canopy. Wayne is naked now, other than white socks and a pair of puppy slippers.

Three black jets spurt from the horizon. They arc over the playa as one evil thing. The noise is cruel. One, two, three, four raging passes, then they vanish across the mountain range to the east. If this were a movie, we'd have a mid-air collision, they'd burst into flames, smoking metal would fall from the sky.

"What do you think, man?" says Wayne. "Could we be a more tempting target? Thirty-thousand cultural creatives all in one place and no real buildings to get damaged?"

I squint toward the spot where the jets disappeared. After the jets the techno beat sounds mellow as rain.

"They'd blame it on the terrorists," I say.

"Ashcroft's wet dream," says Wayne.

***

I wake from an afternoon nap swaddled in sweat, doomed to hell by some freaky nightmare and a jackhammering noise that shouldn't be this close to my tent. I try to get out, but the zipper's jammed. I'm in an oven, I'm on my knees, I'm in the direct path of this noise. For all I know, I'm about to be the next sucker to get creamed under the truck tires of some drunk. And still, the demented zipper won't work! I find the knife in my pocket and slash through the door. I tumble out and spring to my feet. Stand free over my wrecked tent. The dry desert air feels cool for a moment as it flows over my wet skin.

Wayne is giving me a hard time from his lawnchair. "Was that necessary?" he says.

Okay. So they've got their generator going full blast at the next camp over. I fold the blade and put my knife back in my jeans. I go sit by Wayne in the shade. Some half-dressed prom queen who calls him or herself Nola is behind Wayne giving him a backrub.

"I was deep into this Clockwork Orangey dream," I say. "I was at a window and a bunch of punks comes roaring up our driveway on motorcycles. They're all black leather and chains."

I continue. "Meanwhile, Melissa comes up from the basement."

"You guys have a basement?" says Wayne. His eyes are closed and his head lolls back into Nola's belly.

"This is a goddamn *dream*," I say. "So Melissa goes out there and I do nothing to stop her. I stand there looking out the window while these maggots get off their bikes and start punching and kicking my daughter to the ground."

"So what'd you do?" says Wayne.

"That's the point," I whine. "I did *nothing*!"

I get up and walk over to the cooler by Wayne's van. I take out a wet bottle, suck down half a beer, return to my lawnchair. "And then I woke up broiling in my tent with a goddamn stuck zipper," I say.

Wayne opens his eyes. "The trick to zippers in this dust," says Wayne, "is to rub them with soap."

"Don't get me started on the dust," says Nola, still kneading Wayne's back. "I brought my saxophone out here once? It cost me nine hundred dollars to get it cleaned." Nola makes mournful eyes under fake eyelashes.

"They're saying on the news that dust is the reason why things aren't working in Iraq," I say.

"I thought it was sand," says Wayne.

"I thought it was American Imperialism," says Nola.

The sun roasts across my back. I edge my lawnchair into the shrinking patch of shade, to where my knees are almost touching Wayne's. I lean forward with both my hands wrapped hard around the beer bottle.

"Tell me your honest opinion," I say. "You know how Melissa is. If a tank were headed for her tent, do you think she'd slash her way out?"

Wayne gives me a look.

"If her zipper were stuck!" I yell.

"Man, you are seriously tweaking," says Wayne.

"I mean this is a girl who washes and recycles those plastic bags you put your lettuce in. This is a girl who does *mending*." I drop my empty beer bottle to the ground and slap my hand against the right knee of my pants. "Check it out," I say.

Wayne leans over. His shoulders slip free of Nola's hands, which immediately go to adjusting his or her platinum wig and rhinestone tiara. Wayne examines the tidy little stitches along the edge of my knee patch.

"See what I mean?" I say. "Don't you think a girl like Melissa would *hesitate* before slashing her way out of a tent?"

Wayne leaves his hand on my knee. "Steve," he says.

"What?" I say.

"Listen to me, bro." Wayne tightens his hold on my knee. "Your kid in Iraq?" he says. "That's not your fault."

***

And then later that night I see Melissa, her long hair flamboyant in the wind. She's seated on a chariot that's spurting blue-green fire from a couple of flame-throwers. I run after her until the chariot is lost in the overall chaos and illumination.

Wait a minute, wasn't there a phone call? A phone call where Melissa told me she had cut her hair.

No way could her hair grow back so soon.

And now I see that I've done it again, lost my bearings in the neon roar of Black Rock City at night, lost Wayne and Nola and the entire band of pilgrims I started the evening with.

Yes, this is something I now remember. Melissa left her amazing hennaed hair at some training camp in Texas.

I pull up the sarong at my waist, it keeps trying to fall off, this flimsy piece of cloth that Nola talked me into when it was too hot for anything else. But now the world is coming unraveled in this wind, and I'm cold and clueless as to how to get back to camp. All I can do is wander from fire to fire and search for something familiar in the shadowy faces of strangers.

Until, between fires, I get hit by a dust devil. It funnels me into the mouth of a windsock tube, I push through a curtain of blowing fabric into the pulsing soundtrack of a large tent, and now I'm in the smoky red haze of some kind of club that smells of incense and burnt hair. I rub grit from my eyes and behold half-naked people in shackles on the ground. A girl in handcuffs, a guy in chains, someone else holding something that might be a cattle prod.

"Master or slave?" says a man's voice near my ear. A woman covered in tattoos approaches me smiling.

"Not my thing," I say. I tighten the knot on my sarong and back out the door. "But hey," I say, "I can feel the love."

And it's true, even in there.

***

A bunch of early risers, or those of us who never went to bed, are waiting in line for bags of ice. Even at this hour, the playa still pulses to the beat, some techno trance DJ working the morning. Next to me in line is a woman holding a parasol. She's got the well-rested look of a morning person. And here is a guy wandering around spray-painted purple. His cock dangles loose between his legs. This guy's cock is so big it makes me want to get a tape measure. I'd hate to see it hard. Meanwhile all of us ordinary citizens get to imagine what he does with it at night. We get to stare at this purple thing from behind our mirror sunglasses.

Except for the woman with the parasol; she slides her sunglasses down to the tip of her nose and gives herself an eyefull. Her long gauzy dress, her pale protected skin, the shape of her nose in profile; if this were a movie she'd be Meryl Streep.

The woman notices me noticing her in the ice line and both of us noticing the purple cock.

We're having a moment.

And now she winks at me, pushes the sunglasses back up her nose, and lifts her parasol so its shade covers us both. We move forward with the ice line as if we were a couple. I offer to take a turn holding the parasol. Behind us, the subject is Burning Man art.

"Dude, what's with all the *religious* bullshit?"

"Yeah, one more temple and I'm gonna puke."

"It's not about religion," says a girl's voice. "It's spiritual."

"Same thing."

"No it's not."

"Well, whatever, it's not art."

"Oh, these kids," whispers the woman, as if we shared such insights all the time. She turns to look at them, and I shift the shade of the parasol so it covers her face.

"Ya'll want to know art?" says the woman. Her voice is spiced by some kind of Deep South.

"Sure," says a girl with dirt-colored dreads. They've all got metal doodads hung from various body parts.

The woman lifts her sunglasses to the top of her head and squints into the naked light. She's older this way, the creases around her eyes, but I'd follow her as far as she'd let me across this hopeless desert. Just holding her parasol, and I'm cured of being a tourist.

"Nine 'leven," says the woman in her adorable accent. "Now *tha-yut* was a work of art."

The air throbs. Serpentine sounds spiral around the subwoofer heartbeat. No one says a word. And I'm not sure what undoes me more – the woman's words or the eerie sense that we all know exactly what she's saying.

***

High noon on Wayne's bike and I'm rolling a straight line toward the temple. The temple floats on waves of heat in the distance, its watery onion-shaped minarets spiking the sky. Between me and the temple a lone man stands in his shadow on the empty playa. He won't give an inch as I approach, so I swerve around him at the last moment and see that he's pissing. He could be playa art, an installation titled, "Man Who Thinks He Can Piss a Hole to China."

As if I haven't drilled a few holes into the playa myself.

The temple turns out to be a good place to escape the sun. I hang out under its shade and read the graffiti. The graffiti on the walls is a bunch of prayers and poems and apologies, all about dead people. Photographs are taped up and down the columns and walls. A studio portrait of an old couple. A guy on a snowboard suspended in a deep blue sky. And here's a middle-aged woman with pigtails and a backwards baseball cap. Someone's mom, too cute to be dead.

One useful thing I could write about Melissa's mom is that she might have been more careful about avoiding the sun or at least used sunscreen.

If Melissa were here she'd want to put up a picture. Melissa has all the pictures I never took of her mom. Linda and I tanked too early for pictures, too early to have anything between us but the baby in her belly. And when Linda got on a plane to Hawaii, six months pregnant, that was the end of that. Linda kept Melissa to herself for twelve years and then she died and I got Melissa and Melissa got nothing but a bunch of pictures of Linda posing on various beaches. Whichever photos Melissa didn't take to Iraq must be in boxes with the rest of the stuff she packed away before deployment.

Deployment. Now there's a word.

I tried to stop her. I found my daughter turning her room upside down, a clutter of boxes, books, and clothes. She was sitting on the floor surrounded by a platoon of stuffed animals. “You don’t need to do this,” I said from the doorway.

“Yes I do,” said Melissa. “I want you to make this room back into a studio, how it was before I came to live with you. You should get back into clay. Get back into your art.”

“Fuck art,” I said. “If I hadn’t wasted my time with art, I might have earned us some money to put you through college.”

Melissa made a nest of white tissue paper in a cardboard box. She put in her beanie babies and taped shut the box.

“You’re not going to do this,” I said. I went in and sat on the bed. “Now that you’re all packed,” I said, “we can move to Canada.”

“Dad,” she said. Melissa never called me dad, up until then I’d only been Steve to her. This new word scared me. She must have seen it in my face, she reached out her hand and touched my foot.

“Dad,” she said, “this isn’t the sixties.”

The things I could write on these walls about Melissa if I were the type. If I thought it could make a difference.

And now I notice the fat magic marker abandoned on a bench. I go pick it up. Pop the cap and have a sniff. The sudden hit of fumes comes as a surprise, I expected it to have gone dry.

Forget it, this so-called Temple of Honor with its filigreed remembrances has nothing to do with me or my hellbent daughter. And my Melissa is not dead. My Melissa is alive, either in or outside of Baghdad.

Jesus Christ, Baghdad.

And now I see the man who seduced my daughter. His stiff back, his clean-shaved face, his stuffed jacket with its insignia and brass. He called it an open door to higher education. He called it a chance to see the world. He called it a peacetime army.

I bite the plastic cap between my teeth. Hold the black magic marker like a knife ready to stab someone in the heart. I write these slanted words on the temple wall: STAFF SERGEANT CLIFF HOSKINS, US ARMY 6th RECRUITING BRIGADE, YOU LOUSY LYING

HEADHUNTER. MAY IT BE YOUR CHILD IN PLACE OF MINE.

***

What was I thinking?

I headed off into the darkness after sampling at a bunch of free bars, and now I'm flat in the moonless middle of nowhere. I try to cover myself with what's left of Nola's sarong after I cut it loose from the bike chain. I hold a tassle to my heart and roll myself up like a burrito. I turn my face toward the lights of Black Rock City juking on the horizon, and I look north of the city to where the Man stands alone, a blue neon colossus on top of a pyramid. And up here we have Mars overhead, pulsing in a trance dance of its very own.

Does Melissa know it's been sixty or so thousand years since Mars has come this close?

And does the Iraqi desert have such winds? Does the Iraqi night get so cold?

Coming toward me are a distant pair of headlights, closer and closer until I'm nailed in the blinding beam.

"Sorry, dude," says a voice, and the lights go out. I drop my hands from my face. It turns out to be just a couple of rangers on patrol in a jeep. They get out with their flashlights, and now I have to convey to these kids in Utilikilts that I'm not another E-tard they need to scrape from the playa and deliver to medical camp. They give the standard lecture about dehydration and leave me a tall bottle of water, along with a nice fleece blanket.

I fall asleep, weepy with love for these young heroes.

And wake up tilting toward the blue light of morning. I may be cheek-to-cheek with the playa, but I'm still losing my balance. The beat of some all night rave comes and goes, as elastic as the wind. Black Rock City growls with the rumble of a few thousand generators.

Things have been going on in this way for about a week now. Just one simple moment of silence, is that asking too much?

I manage to get up on one elbow and suckle water from the bottle, then fall to my back while the sky gets an infusion of sunrise. This is going to be one hell of a morning after. I'm shivering with cold and my body feels like someone rolled over it with a tank. I remember something I overheard about a hotspring pool in an oasis of green, hidden somewhere on the edge of this desert. That is absolutely the place to be right now.

I drag my sorry ass off the ground and huddle into my blanket of fleece, stumble barefoot across the playa. Stretched out before my toes is a long skinny Arab in a bhurka.

At least my shadow knows where we're going.

But those distant mountains don't get any closer. My shadow shrivels into this desiccated little blob under my feet. I abandon my blanket to the heat. The wind steals the sarong. And now comes vomiting, diarrhea, thirst. My water's gone.

The devil knows this wouldn't be the first time some idiot wandered off naked and alone to die in the desert. But who am I fooling? I know I'm faking it. I know I won't die out here, I know I'll be rescued by the next patrol of Black Rock Rangers. Yet here I am staging some cliché movie where I get to stand at the intersection of Heaven and Hell and make my deal with God.

I fall to my knees in my ridiculous little shadow, I play out my part. Okay, God, here's the deal: deploy *me* to the wasteland. You know what I'm saying here.

***

Early evening and Mary Magdalena has pulled her mobile footwash cart into our camp. I'm wrecked in my lawnchair, fresh from mainlining saltwater at medical. Three hours of soothing IV. And now my filthy cracked feet are in the hands of this sweet-breasted girl. Like everything else around here, Mary's hands guide me into some strange melding of pleasure and pain. Meanwhile Wayne, Nola, and a bunch of Germans with names too weird to remember are all getting glitzed and glittered for the big burn. Between costume changes, they're all toking this and snorting that.

At least they don't try to suck me into their scene. Other than Nola batting his or her eyelashes my way. Nola, who found and delivered Mary Magdalena. I give Nola a thumbs up, and even though it's not my thing, I blow Nola a kiss.

But back to Mary Magdalena. She kneels before me on a small mud-caked carpet. Her shape is elfin, I can see it all through her transparent green gown. Narrow hips like a boy, girlish breasts that may or may not be done growing, pubes shaved into a Mohawk. She pours cool water from a plastic jug over my feet, which sets off a whole new wave of whatever it is, pleasure, pain. The water runs muddy into a green Rubbermaid. She works over my feet with a wet washcloth, dries them with a frayed towel. Now she rubs in scented oil, pulls her fingers between my toes. Her fingernails are tipped with black crescents of dirt and this is where I loose it, this is where I tilt from giddy to something else. I close my eyes tight, but it's too late, I'm already pierced by those beautiful black crescents of dirt tracing the fingernails of Mary Magdalena. I close my throat, but something squeaks out.

"It's okay," says Mary. She gives my foot a comforting squeeze.

But no, it's not okay. It is not okay to turn into the statue of a father when my child tells me she's in the army and then go all blubbery at the sight of some little mama's dirty fingernails. It is not okay to lose myself in the kindness of strangers while the devil knows what cruelties await my daughter. It is not okay to feel the love in the middle of some hedonistic party while the one person who matters falls into the fires of hell.

"It's okay," says Mary Magdalena. She holds my foot quite still in her hand. She looks up from where she's kneeling, her eyes completely open to mine, and I see that she's holding me and my foot hostage. I see that she will not let go until I do. I see what she's up to, how she's waiting for me to surrender to the magical power of reflexology or whatever it is she wants to believe in.

Oh, these kids.

And this is the last thought before I give way to what she wants. Oh these kids, and now I'm crying and now I'm gone and now this crying is something that is happening without me.

After the crying comes a calm where Mary Magdalena and I are nothing but eyes watching each other. Then I remember myself, I knuckle my eyes. "They dosed me with two bags of saltwater," I say. "It looks like they went over the fill line."

Mary goes back to work. She puts down my foot and pulls a tube of chapstick from a beaded bag at her waist. She removes the cap and twists the tube. She holds the foot back up and says, "This one needs a little something extra, it's cracked deep." She rubs chapstick into the ravine on my heel.

And I title this piece, "Girl Who Attends to Man's Cracked Sole."

***

Nola has used his or her pull to get us on the crowded upper deck of *La Contessa*. This is a tall Spanish galleon now rolling to a stop behind a ring of thirty thousand people. Everyone down on the playa is going crazy. They're wearing glow sticks and blinky things that bob up and down with the drumbeat.

"They've got enough naked fire dancers down there to populate their own planet," someone says.

"Enough drum power to wake up the snakes in Washington," says someone else.

From up here on *La Contessa*, the night is spread out like a sacrificial offering. And here's the centerpiece, the Man, this blue neon deity who stands on top of a pretentious pyramid and towers over the whole scene.

"You wanna know how all this started?" says a guy who's pressed against the wooden rail next to me. I don't know if he's talking to me or to someone else, there's such a crush of bodies up here in the dark. But his voice goes on, one voice among the many. "Some dude's girlfriend ditched him for another guy, I think it was his best friend. So the dude has a party. He builds a wooden statue of the guy who stole his chick, and he burns this statue on the beach, and everyone digs it, so the dude does it again every summer until there's so many folks coming they get kicked off the beach."

Something is changing about the Man. He's lifting his arm, he's growing a bright red heart.

"Born out of pain," says the guy, "the untold history of Burning Man."

"Well, you just told it, honey," says Nola's voice, from my other side on the rail.

The Man now has a red cartoon heart that's throbbing in time. This is something new, this brilliant red heart in the center of the Man's blue neon ribs. And now we have rockets and fireworks and explosions. The pyramid ignites into flames, the crowd screams its head off as the Man is shot through with fire, even as his heart is keeping the beat. And everyone's shouting like *they* did this, myself included. We're all pyromaniacs at heart.

And then later, after the Man has fallen, after the party has moved back into Black Rock City, Nola and Wayne walk, one on each side of me, as I limp back to camp. We skirt around the acres of burning rubble, and I say, "Just think about Baghdad."

Wayne sighs. He doesn't want to think about Baghdad. He doesn't want me to think about Baghdad. Wayne brought me here to take my mind off Baghdad.

"Flames, cacophony, and chaos," says Nola.

It's all I can do not to go weepy again, that Nola is willing to think about Baghdad.

"The difference is," Nola goes on, "the difference is that *these* people have no interest in killing each other."

And we walk on across the dark playa, no longer sure of our direction, because with the Man burned down, there's nothing but Mars to use for navigation.

A Typical Wednesday

Richard Dunford

I walk to the bathroom noticing I've put on a little weight. I stand in different poses in the mirror but can't shift the flab. I do some sit-ups.

I clean my teeth twice, yes twice, then knock one out thinking about some fat waitress who served me. I never fantasize about women I want to have sex with; what if the real thing isn't as good.

I kiss my wife, dead to the world in bed, then leave.

Skip to the doctors.

I sit in the surgery waiting room filled with elderly people and screaming children patiently waiting to see someone else's doctor.

The doctor gives me a full medical examination. His finger up my bum makes me feel socially uncomfortable.

On the way to my buddy Nate's office I notice a shop with a 50% off sale.

I consider myself a good person.

I take a lift up to his floor sharing the elevator with a woman who smells of tuna and has one leg shorter than the other.

Skip to the office.

I pull out a gun with a silencer attached and shoot Nate at point blank range in the face.

He looks surprised.

His bloody lifeless head slumps down on the same glass table on which he had romantically been ramming his loins into my wife's adulterous frame.

I consider myself emotionally unbalanced.

Wait.
Did I really just say that?
What have I done?
… there's a 50% sale on and I almost missed it.

Skip to the end.

The Object of Desire

Jennifer A. Donnelly

The collector's gaze moved from the pedestrians forty-five stories below, mute and remote as dolls, to the torso of a woman recumbent under his hands, bare but for a thin layer of fabric draped over her hips. David contemplated the effect of the afternoon light upon her skin, how the sharp angle of the late autumn rays shadowed the grooves of her ribs, the curve of her breasts, the soft valley of her sternum, the "V" smiling between her thighs. Her wordlessness echoed that of the strangers on the sidewalks, veiled the untold tales spinning in her dreams.

"You must never leave me," David murmured. Her absence would have been palpable, he thought, moving his eyes from her slumbering form over the room's interior. Everything in his apartment – the position of the walls, the arrangement of the furniture – appeared to have been designed to show her figure to the best advantage. The color of the curtains brought out her cheekbones like a stroke of rouge; the texture of the upholstery heightened the tint of her complexion. Even the sculptures installed throughout this room and the halls visible beyond paid tribute as though she were their queen. There, his glance paused. *My collection.*

In addition to the marble sculptures on pedestals, which were nearly life-sized, smaller figurines and statuettes in terracotta and semi-precious stones were mounted in glass cases and an amphora painted with red figures was displayed in a corner. A large mosaic was fitted with a base so that it stood up like a table; atop a sheet of protective glass, a tiny copper easel supported a chipped bit of clay that on closer inspection revealed traces of color – the fragment of a painting. All that remained of a fresco that once filled an entire wall in Crete was this single kohl-lined eye peering out from a spiral of ebony curls.

The richness and variety of the collection gave the apartment the feel of a nest woven with great attention, over much time. And so it had been: almost twenty years had passed since David had come back to the city from New Haven – a different sort of nest, one where discovery was valuable in itself, where proofs could be elegant. In New York, on the other hand, discovery demanded an application, preferably one with monetary gain. Beauty floated through the city's air – the brush of a red elm leaf against a polished jewelry-store window in its slow descent to the sidewalk; the scent of shallots cooking in butter at a French restaurant; the flutter of a ballerina's foot at the Lincoln Center, of which David was a benefactor – but having all this came at a price. The possession of beauty required money.

With this nagging truth in mind, he rose from his armchair. He regretted having to spend the evening at the office, but as he often remarked to his junior associates, "Sunday has the most maddening way of preceding Monday." His face assumed an expression of resignation as he reached to caress the woman's hip one last time before going away. She was beautiful, yes, but obligations were obligations. Leaving her by the window, he gathered his papers and wallet and walked out the door.

*

Though he had only been able to sleep a couple of hours and change into a fresh suit dropped off by the doorman, David was already sitting behind his desk by the time lights began to flicker on in the directors' offices and the juniors' cubicles. He was not tired. He never slept a lot. If he ever finished work at a reasonable hour, he would stay awake until late, looking at his collection or flipping through an auction catalogue. This calmed him.

An important strategy meeting was scheduled for that afternoon with some of the firm's other directors regarding a potential client in France. David didn't dread the meeting – his numbers were ready, his remarks prepared – but all the same, he wasn't looking forward to the long hours with the frowns that invariably surrounded the gleaming walnut conference table. He often tried to break the tension with small jokes – he was partial to wordplays – but his colleagues never so much as cracked a smile. Luckily, however, a midday appointment glimmered in the center of his antique silver desk calendar – a light *between* tunnels, he mused: lunch with Vasilevo, an antiquities dealer from whom he had been buying for years.

Vasilevo's network of sellers and buyers was particularly strong from Macedonia to the Middle East, though it drew upon all the lands touching the Mediterranean. His expertise on sculpture ranged from wide-hipped, ample-breasted fertility figures to the decadent, narcissistic nonsense that had somehow passed as art in Europe and America for the past decades. As a teenager he had fled from Skopje, eventually ending up in New York via Moscow and then Paris. His English was still marked with a clipped cadence and a swallowing of consonants.

Around lunchtime David's car picked him up from Rockefeller Center and drove him to the tree-lined streets of Chelsea. A young woman behind the desk smiled when he entered the gallery. Vasilevo's new assistant, he supposed; he hadn't seen her before. Or maybe he had. They all ran together in his mind, these gallerinas: slim in their black pantsuits, with chestnut hair pulled back in chignons and Tiffany silver in their ears. This one was speaking on the telephone, and David was glad to have a moment to look around. A statue in bronze intrigued him by seeming to glow under the spotlights, though he generally preferred marble, alabaster, jade – materials lifted from the earth, rather than forged in some infernal oven.

"Are you Dr. Steinberg?"

David turned; the young woman had gotten up from her desk and was standing beside him.

"Mr. Vasilevo will be here shortly. He arrived from Istanbul this morning and was stuck in customs for hours." Her voice was soothing and polite, as with all gallerinas, but mercifully lacked that cloying tone that suggested "*buy, buy, buy* ...". It was brushed with an accent he couldn't place.

"*Doctor* Steinberg!" He laughed. "Nobody has called me that in years."

She cocked her head. "That's how it was written in the appointment book."

"Wonder where they found that. I try to keep it quiet."

"That's a shame! Why do you do that?"

David looked at the young woman. How to explain, he wondered, the warning he had received at her age – that his doctorate in archaeology would be considered unprofessional, even dangerous, a telltale sign of ambivalence about finance? Would that justify the resolution he had therefore made: to conceal the eight years he had spent sifting soil with pick-axes and paintbrushes, and to forget the ineffable ecstasy of discovering in some pile of dirt a shard of ceramic, a carved bit of stone?

"It has no relevance any more," he smiled. "Please, don't call me Dr. Steinberg. It makes me feel very old. My name is David."

"I'm Susanna."

As they shook hands, Vasilevo walked into his gallery, dressed as always in a black suit and white shirt that set off his blue eyes and silver hair. He showed no signs of fatigue from his journey.

"I see you have met my niece," he rasped. "Come, we have much to discuss."

*

Late that night, following an interminable strategy meeting that had dragged on into a tedious dinner of steaks and Bordeaux, David sat awake next to his lovely companion, worrying. The following evening he would be in a plane bound for Paris, but this didn't bother him: seducing a potential client was a relatively straightforward process, and his secretary would ensure that the hotel placed in his room the fresh suit and toiletries he kept there for these last-minute trips.

What troubled him was the proposition Vasilevo had made over lunch, regarding the best piece in David's collection: his statue of the goddess Artemis, which was in exceptional condition, having retained its head, both legs, and one arm despite centuries submerged in the Adriatic. Actually, the long wash of the salt water had lent the marble a frothy texture and an almost metallic shimmer that rendered the piece quite unlike any other of its kind. On this last trip around the Mediterranean, Vasilevo had explained, he had been reminded just how difficult political unrest and clamors for repatriation were making it to obtain authentic, high-quality antiquities. Thus, the value of David's piece was many times what he had paid two decades before, and if he would allow Vasilevo to sell it, there would be substantial profit for both of them.

David had grown so accustomed to seeing the statue in his home, greeting him when he returned from work, that he never thought of its monetary value or its interest for the outside world. *Could* he part with it, or with any of the other statues? His eyes scanned the pedestals and shelves, trying to imagine them empty. The exercise was disheartening; each work told a story, not only of its maker, its materials, its provenance, but of how he had obtained it, and where, and for what price.

Artemis, for example, had been bought for a song from construction workers digging the foundation for a shopping center while David was doing his final doctoral research. By returning to the United States through Africa and South America, he had managed to skirt customs and keep the statue. He had imagined installing it in the foyer of the house in New Haven that he and his fiancée had looked at together before he had left for Europe a few weeks earlier. He already had an offer to become a tenure-track associate professor, while she hoped eventually to advance from curator to director of the university gallery. When he walked into their apartment on his return from Europe, she was still in bed with his advisor.

Soon thereafter, when he had completed his dissertation, David paid a visit to his uncle, the one who at family get-togethers invariably thumped him on the back and said, "There's always a place in our bank for bright young people like yourself, no matter what they may have chosen to study." During those first years at the bank he had worked around the clock, trying to master the new field as well as fend off rumors of nepotism. It paid off, and as his professional success increased, so did his appetite for buying sculptures, whose solid, tangible presence proved soothing after a day of dry financial analyses and often tense negotiations. After a while, he no longer could say whether he bought the statues to clear his head for work or whether he worked in order to buy more statues.

"I'd have to do some serious thought before selling," he had told Vasilevo that afternoon.

The sun had long since gone down; in only a few hours it would rise again, casting its yellow-orange haze over the New York sky. David changed into pajamas and crawled into bed with a catalogue of Cycladic figurines, their breasts and hips curved precisely like violins, but millennia before the instrument was invented – a mystery he loved to ponder. He gazed at one of the flat, moonlike faces. His lids became heavy, and as they started to fall, the statue's face metamorphosed into that of Vasilevo's niece, Susanna.

"Sleep," she whispered. He obeyed.

*

During the night David dreamed of the statue of Artemis and awoke disoriented. He resolved to talk with Vasilevo before leaving for Paris that evening. His secretary scheduled his car early so he could stop by the gallery on the way to the airport. On his way out of the office he stopped by the restroom and studied his reflection in the mirror: ashen rings under the eyes, a yellow tint on the teeth from years of smoking. And my skin, he remarked, is a ghastly shade of green under these fluorescent lights. He ran some water over his hands and slicked back his hair.

When he arrived at the gallery Susanna was affixing a red sticker to a wall label.

"Mr. Vasilevo won't be back until evening," she said.

"Damn," he replied. "I wanted to see him before I left."

"Can I give him a message?"

"It's a matter I need to discuss with him myself. Does he have some time on Friday? I'll be back in the city by then."

"Is twelve o'clock fine?" she asked. "Where are you going?"

"Paris."

"I wish I was going to Paris!" She beamed. "I used to study at the Ecole des Beaux-Arts, before I came to New York."

"Well, I'd gladly have you go in my place." What a contrast Susanna's liveliness made with the calculated impassivity of his partners, David sighed; she must be the same age as my junior associates, those specters of boys on the fast track to becoming hollow men, like me. But she, David thought, still has enthusiasm, and it seems to mask neither insincerity nor vapidity. His mind returned to a memory that had been sparked the day before: himself aged twenty-four, wearing his dig khakis.

"I'll bring you something."

"You are very kind," Susanna smiled, "but just have fun. And give my greetings to the Beaux-Arts."

There would be little fun in his forty-eight hours in Paris, David assured her. As the plane left the runway, he considered: all the same, I will bring something from Paris for Susanna.

*

"*Ça vaut le voyage*," David smiled as he walked out of his new client's offices in Paris. They had closed the deal, which meant great things financially for all concerned – his partners, the client, and, of course, himself. It was early afternoon. Soon his colleagues in New York would be filing into their offices, and he would need to speak with them; in the early evening, he would meet the client again to sign the contract over dinner. He had exactly one hour for himself.

"Ecole des Beaux-Arts," he told the driver.

The car drove down Avenue Montaigne, past ladies peering into the windows of boutiques at mannequins wearing the winter collections, and crossed the Seine on a bridge crowned with gilded sea goddesses. Armed policemen and haughty statues stood sentinel over the statesmen inside the National Assembly, where the car turned onto Boulevard Saint Germain. David got out of the car before the wrought-iron gates of the art school and stepped into a courtyard paved with wide stones. At the far end a row of arched windows alternated with tall casts of classical sculptures: a slim youth, naked but for sandals and a cloak; a deity or maiden, also stripped bare; a hero forcing the Gorgon's head he held with one muscled arm to look at herself in the mirror he held in the other. To the right, a sign indicated a display of student work in the presence of the artists. He followed the arrow to an exhibition hall.

Natural light from an unseen window was streaming onto walls hung with paintings, sketches, and photographs. In enclosed spaces televisions showed what he had learned to call "installations", displays of video and sound and deliberately incongruous objects lying around. In his business suit and overcoat David felt out of place among the student artists speaking with studied aloofness to mostly dishevelled visitors. He was about to ask if there was a gift shop when he noticed a small display case holding bronze and plaster casts from a young woman's body: a pair of hands, a sculpted foot, the side of a face. Disembodied, isolated, the pieces reminded David of fragments of an excavated statue.

"Are these yours?" he asked the young man standing next to the case.

"I made them," he replied. His fingers toyed with a pouch of tobacco.

David's eyes fell upon a hollow cast of the young woman's back. Her unrepresented legs must have been dipping into an arabesque: the small of the back curved sharply to one side, the fine muscles were knitted like lace around the bones. Her personality spoke through the bronze – delicate, but strong.

"That is my girlfriend." The student nodded at the piece.

"You're very talented," David said.

The student shrugged. "My teacher says this is not art, because I mold the plaster onto the model. He says it is not original." He was rolling a cigarette. "But the people buy these, not the experimentations we make in class. I sold already three."

David took a lighter from his pocket and lit the young man's cigarette. He looked at the other pieces, each one representing some aspect of an individual that the young artist had known or met, loved or hated, attempted to understand and recreate in plaster, wax, and bronze.

"I would like to buy something," he said.

The student looked up at him with interest. "These have to stay here in the exposition," he replied, "but I have more in my studio." He scribbled a number on a scrap of paper.

"I will come tomorrow," David said. He started to walk out, then stopped and turned back to the student.

"Don't ever sell the girl."

*

At noon on Friday, David was sitting in Vasilevo's gallery in New York.

"I won't sell."

The dealer replied quickly. "The entire profit will go to you. The gallery won't take its cut."

The offer was generous – unheard of, David knew; but he didn't need the money, particularly after this deal in Paris.

"I have grown too used to the statue," he told the dealer.

Vasilevo appeared thoughtful. "You know, we might consider making a cast. Louis Quatorze lined the drive into Versailles with copies of Greek and Roman statues."

"But the copy would not be the original," David replied. "Anyway, I can't stand the idea of her being installed in someone else's home. Or even worse, in a museum, to be ogled at by everyone who walks by. And the thought of seeing her in the gallery or on the auction block, being put to sale, like a –" David stopped, grimacing. "It just seems indecent."

Vasilevo was no longer looking at David but at a Byzantine Madonna on the wall, her gilded, almost oriental eyes drooping at the corners.

"What could possibly persuade you?" He asked sadly.

"I don't know that anything could," David replied.

Susanna's desk was empty when David walked out of Vasilevo's office into the main gallery, but he took a moment to scribble a note and tuck it under the telephone before getting into his waiting car.

*

That night, David sat behind his desk at the office, shuffling through spreadsheets: the rigid grid of columns and rows, the regular curves of numbers and symbols, seemed a map, an atlas, a calculated topography of an invisible world, the world of money ... the black ink blurred onto the white paper, became a sheet of graph paper corresponding to a made grid of string over a patch of soil, and he was on an archaeological dig by the sea. Every object he found was measured and catalogued, its precise coordinates were plotted using the grid and the graph paper – which also made a map, a plan, a collection of histories, of a world that had been crushed, scattered, buried for millennia until some chance wanderer should uncover them and put them back together, giving new life and –

David jolted awake. When had he drifted off?

He looked out at the "cube farm", as the junior associates called it; the field of desks and half-walls where they stared at computer screens late on a Friday night, creases of overwork starting at the corners of their eyes. They should be taking their girlfriends to the movies, David thought, or watching football with college friends. He stood up and walked out to the cubicles.

"Should we call it a night?" He heard himself say.

*

On Saturday afternoon David was waiting outside the Frick Collection when he saw Susanna turn from Fifth Avenue onto East 70th Street. She was not dressed in her gallerina black, but in faded jeans, a sweater, and a knit cap with a pompon. In the sun, away from the spotlights and ambient bulbs of the gallery, her hair was copper, and it fell around her shoulders in unbrushed curls. David wished they could linger awhile among the sculpted branches of the topiary garden.

"Thank you for coming," he said, and she smiled in response as they climbed the steps to the arched doorway. They crossed the marble foyer and entered an oak-paneled room in which a docent was lecturing a concertedly serious group of visitors.

"In the context of Henry Clay Frick's home, works such as Fragonard's *The Progress of Love,"* her voice droned, indicating four paintings of a much-powdered man courting a satin-decked lady, "transcend their isolated epistemological relevance by testifying to the aesthetic psyche of early twentieth-century collectors ..."

"I like this place," Susanna said. "It's like being at someone's tea party." The couple walked through the ballroom and the library, between walls covered in crushed velvet and hung with varnished oils, past vases of porcelain and earthenware, an oak commode veneered with panels of tulipwood. Central Park was always audible, but hidden behind the brocade curtains. In a dressing room, their gazes fell upon a portrait of a distinguished gentleman in a dark overcoat and cashmere scarf, framed in gilt wood, presiding over the treasures in the room.

"Look," Susanna whispered, "it's you." David's reflection in the mirror could indeed have been that of Mr. Frick himself. David stepped aside and the gentleman disappeared.

"Now you," he said to Susanna, and as he guided her forward her image appeared in the gold frame. She laughed.

"I remember when my uncle took me to the Hermitage, I told him that my doll wanted the tsarina's crown."

"Did she get it?"

"My uncle told me the things in museums aren't for sale. So I decided that someday I'd go work in one."

They meandered into a glass-domed courtyard and sat on a bench among the orchids and ferns by a fountain statue of a winged nymph poised for flight, its expression a mixture of capriciousness and wisdom.

David produced a small package from his overcoat and gave it to Susanna. He watched rapt as she hesitantly unwrapped the layers of tissue to reveal a pair of hands in plaster, as her fingers stroked the molded palms.

"I hate that in museums you can't touch the objects," she said. "At the gallery my uncle is always yelling at me for putting my hands on things."

"With your own art, you can do whatever you want," said David.

"I never had any. Just slides and photographs." Susanna looked up. "What's it like to own art?"

David looked at Susanna's fingers laced around those of the sculpture, which reached into the air, grasping at something unseen. Some powdery residue had gotten onto her wrists. As he reached over to brush it off, he noticed the greyish hue of his skin next to hers.

"Why don't you see for yourself?" he said.

*

Sunday morning Susanna lay on her side, her hip curved up toward the ceiling, her elbows bent around the waves of her hair, her chin turned toward the pillow, revealing the edge of an enigmatic smile. She slept soundlessly, utterly still. It was very early. David got up quietly from the bed.

And as he tiptoed down the corridor leading into the living room he caught out of the corner of his eye a glimpse of a woman's shape standing unmoving by the window – he blinked – but there it remained, the unmistakable silhouette of the other, his companion of all these years.

He had forgotten to expect her. He could not utter a word but could only return the accusing stare of his marble goddess, his carved beauty, the Artemis from the Adriatic.

"What's it like to own art?" Susanna had asked him. And so he had shown her the skin cold as the grave, the mouths silent as the dead. And Susanna, as if to mock the immobility of his sculptures, had shown herself warm, loud, dancing, vital; she had kicked open a door that had been overgrown and forgotten to reveal rooms filled with treasures and light.

Maybe – he let the idea creep over him gradually, savoring each nuance of the revelation – there was another way.

He picked up the telephone and dialed a familiar number. Vasilevo answered curtly, still asleep.

"The statue of Artemis is yours," David whispered into the receiver.

At the end of the corridor through the open bedroom door he could see Susanna, and he smiled at this triumph over the old muse who had for so long occupied his nights.

But as he stood there with the telephone to his ear, some pursuit in Susanna's inaccessible dream caused her to change ever so slightly the position of her knees, and in that instant an inexplicable terror grabbed David and held him paralyzed in its grip, as if he had been turned to stone.

*

On a Sunday afternoon in late December, David stood by his window, looking down on the sidewalks. The holiday shoppers were rushing forward, arms laden with parcels and bags, under evergreen boughs strung between flickering streetlamps. David never minded the onset of winter. Starting then, the days became longer.

He turned away from the busy scene outside and greeted his haven within. His eyes swept over the shelves and display cases and came to rest on the pedestal that used to hold the lovely Artemis. Vasilevo's movers had wrapped her like a mummy in layers of protective gauze before lifting her gently into a crate as a body into a coffin. The auction where she was soon thereafter sold had been like a memorial service, the rising bids and the mentions in the art journals like so many eulogies to her beauty and worth. Yes, she was dead to him now. May she rest in peace.

The first time he saw the empty alcove, his insides churned in disbelief and anger. The following days were among the loneliest in his life. But then, one evening, when he had returned to his building after work, the doorman on duty announced that she had finally arrived from Paris – that he had let her in this afternoon. David nearly flew up to his penthouse, and his hands trembled so much as he unlocked the door that he dropped the keys twice. But on the third try he got in.

There she was, waiting for him, glowing in the dimmed spotlights as if illuminated from inside by some vital mysterious fire: Susanna, naked, forged in black-gold bronze. Just as she had wished, she had been able to return to Paris, and the student at the Beaux-Arts had been paid handsomely from the profits of the sale of Artemis.

"You must never leave me," he murmured, and settled down to gaze at her from his armchair by the window.

Ambition

Clare S. Birchall

I know my therapist thinks I'm all talk, so I try to stay quiet, try to prove her wrong. I'm sitting on her couch, sinking in white and soft pink. Marshmallow living. She prompts me with, "So what have you been working on?" I shrug my shoulders, draw zeros with my toe. But she knows the silence won't last. She arches her eyebrows as if to say *Give it your best shot*.

"I want to direct a movie about a man who always just misses historic events. The opposite of *Forrest Gump*. It'll be an anti-epic, he'll go to Woodstock a week too late and find a muddy plain with a few strung-out hippies." My voice is rising.

"I want to produce a hybrid TV show – a soap opera about a talk show and call it *Soaprah.*" I'm on the edge of the sofa now, sitting up straight, tapping out a tune on my knee.

"I want to make a mockumentary about JFK's real assassin who now runs an Italian restaurant in New Jersey serving anti*patsy*." I slap my thigh with joy.

Then I slump. "You've been out of work for a while now," she says. "How would you feel about getting a regular job?" I scowl and say, "There's no business like no business." She asks me if I've been taking my medication but I tell her that I just can't think of myself as bi-polar. It sounds too much like Eskimo swingers.

The Missing Taxi Man

Tomás O'Beirne

The matter of Danny Farrelly, taxi driver, had started as a run-of-the-mill missing person's case but there was nothing conventional about the way it developed.

He had gone to work as usual on Tuesday morning and on Thursday morning his wife, Dolores, phoned the Gardaí to report him missing. The reason she did not phone sooner was because they had a bit of a row on the Monday night, they had not spoken on Tuesday at breakfast and Dolores thought he might have spent the night with his mother in Rialto. She tried to contact him on Wednesday but there was no answer from his mobile. Several times that day she was on the point of phoning his mother but she kept putting it off and telling herself he was sure to turn up that night. She never got on well with Mrs Farrelly Snr. She did phone her first thing on Thursday morning when he failed to come home on Wednesday night but her mother-in-law hadn't seen him.

On getting Dolores Farrelly's call reporting him missing the Gardaí rang the company for which he worked and they were told the last thing they knew about him he had gone to an address in Leeson Park where a Ms Olsen had booked a taxi for noon on Tuesday. She had said she wanted to go to Stillorgan but the taxi company had no destination address for her.

Garda Sergeant Finbarr Walsh and Garda Aideen O'Neill were assigned to go to Leeson Park and find out if Ms Olsen could help them. Finbarr Walsh was from Cork as his name suggested but he had been stationed in Donnybrook for a number of years and he liked it there. It was relatively quiet with no serial killers, gang warfare nor major threats to public order. The work was, let it be said, routine and boring. In fact this suited Finbarr very well because he liked a well ordered existence and he preferred a humdrum job to one where people might shoot at him.

Aideen O'Neill was from Clondalkin and Donnybrook was her first posting and she had only been there three weeks. The way things were with her she did not expect to be there very much longer. She was practically engaged to Alan Moran who worked in the Financial Services Centre but he was saving up to go to America and that was why he could only take her out twice a week.

It was a pleasant, sunny June morning and Aideen who had never been on Leeson Park before was impressed with its prosperous character and she wondered if she and Alan would be able to live in a place like it in the States. Having climbed the steps to Ms Olsen's hall door and rung the bell they were able to admire the well treed road and the neo-Gothic spire of the church opposite them. It was a scene of affluent and sober tranquillity. This tranquillity was dramatically shattered when the door was flung open by a small dark haired lady of between forty and forty-five in a white towelling dressing gown.

'Thank God you're here!' she screamed, 'Come in quick!' and she went dancing down the hall in her bare feet. Climbing the stairs two at a time she suddenly stopped halfway up and said 'You're just in time. She always locks it when she goes out. She knows I'll want to pee if I drink. But I drink anyway. Hurry, Hurry!'

Motioning for Aideen to stay down in the hall Finbarr climbed up to the half landing where the woman was hopping from one foot to the other. 'In there,' she said pointing to a closed door. Acutely aware that it was not the job of Garda Sergeants to pick locks, Finbarr's sense of chivalry still prevailed and he knelt down and started to poke at the lock with his pen knife.

'This is marvellous,' he heard the woman behind him saying. 'When she gets home and sees the door open and everything shipshape the joke will be on her. Ha! Ha! Ha! Yes the joke will be ... Oh dear! It's too late I'm afraid. Oh dear.' He looked around. The woman was squatting down urinating on the expensively carpeted landing.

'She'll be cross with me when she gets back. Very cross. Very, very cross. Yes, I'll be punished for this.'

He finished picking the lock and he swung the door open on what turned out to be a very large, well appointed bathroom whose dominant colour was duck egg blue.

'Thank you kind sir,' she said as she tripped past him leaving the door open behind her. He descended slowly to the hall where Garda O'Neill was red faced from suppressing the laughter that was within her. Wait till I tell this one to the girls, she thought. Finbarr thought she was thinking something like that and it did not amuse him at all.

Aideen liked Finbarr Walsh. She liked him better than most of the others. He was always nice and polite to her, holding doors open and that. In spite of the fact she knew he was married and had children, although she had never met them, she always felt he was uncomfortable in the company of women. He talked all right but it seemed to be a big effort for him.

The image of him kneeling down picking the lock and then turning around and seeing the woman squatting there peeing was one that would remain with her for a very long time. It was so incongruous.

'I'm Garda Sergeant Walsh and this is Garda O'Neill,' Finbarr said when the woman came down. He held his identification for her to see but she waved it away as being of no importance to her.

'You'll have to forgive me for all that trouble I put you to. You almost saved me.'

She smiled a sweet smile up at Finbarr when she said that. She had put on some lipstick and she had straightened her dark brown hair which she wore piled high on her head. Finbarr realised that she was younger than he first thought, perhaps in her early thirties, and she was quite an attractive-looking woman after all but in an off-beat sort of way.

'It was all her fault really. But let's forget about that and have a nice drink.' She darted into the front room without waiting for them to say anything.

The high-ceilinged room had an expansive view of the road outside and the church opposite and the folding doors that led to the back room were open. Both rooms were expensively decorated and furnished in irreproachable good taste. They constituted an excellent example of interior design rectitude which is to say the rooms would have been numbingly characterless if it had not been for the bottles. Apart from the drinks trolley which contained bottles of every imaginable type of out-of-the-way alcohol there were bottles of more conventional spirits sprinkled all over the place. There was a whiskey bottle on the mantlepiece, a vodka bottle in the fireplace, a brandy bottle on the window sill, a gin bottle on the piano and many more besides. Some were nearly empty and some were still nearly full.

'We have quite a good selection,' she said unnecessarily as she made an extravagant gesture encompassing the whole room. 'But I must warn you we have no tonic, not a drop I'm afraid. Olga will have some when she gets back.'

'Thank you but we can't drink on duty. You see ...'

'But you've done your duty. Of course you can drink!'

'I'm sorry Ms Olsen we ...'

'Christ Almighty, I'm not Ms Olsen' she screamed. 'For God sake! Why did you call me Ms Olsen? Do you think I look like her? Do you? You don't think Ms Olsen goes around pissing on the floor? Or is that what you do think? Is that why you called? You thought you'd see Ms Olsen piddling. My God if she thought you thought that about her you'd be for it. She'd punish you so she would. She'll punish me for doing it when she comes in.' Then brightening up she added 'She might punish us all together. Wouldn't that be dreamy?'

'Look Ms, I'm fierce sorry for thinking you were Ms Olsen. You see ...'

'Punish us all together at the same time.' Ignoring him she had her eyes closed when she said this. Then opening them she did a little dance around the room ending up beside the bookcase. She removed a copy of de Sade's *Justine* and reaching into the gap thus formed she extracted a glass containing what looked like tomato juice.

'Cheers,' she said, holding the glass up high. 'I love drinking Bloody Marys in the morning. They make me feel clean and healthy.'

She took a sip from the glass and came tripping back down the room. She's very light on her feet, Finbarr thought and wondered if she was a dancer. She's not a ballet dancer he knew because they are tall and skinny not small and cuddly. She finished her tripping by alighting in the centre of the pliant sofa where she immediately took up the lotus pose.

Perhaps she's a yoga instructor, Finbarr thought but dismissed that notion too on the grounds that Bloody Marys in the morning did not seem compatible with yoga.

'Could we have your real name please?' Aideen spoke for the first time, pencil and notebook at the ready.

'Guess!'

'Guess your name? I can't do that. How could I?'

'Of course you could. Go on. Just concentrate deeply.'

'Come on. We are just wasting time,' Finbarr interjected, who thought she was now behaving as if she was in her early twenties.

'All right. I'll tell you. I'm Little Lilly. Now you could have guessed that couldn't you? You weren't prepared to concentrate. Nobody is prepared to concentrate any more.'

'What's your second name?' Aideen asked.

'I told you. It's Lilly! Ha, ha. I bet you really meant what's your third name.'

'O.K. What's your third name?'

'It's Small. I'm Little Lilly Small. Are you sure you won't have a drink? There's loads of Bloody Mary or anything else you want.' She opened the coal scuttle and took out a large jug of red liquid with slices of lemon floating around in it. She refilled her glass, took a sip and sighed contentedly.

'Is that how you sign your cheques? Little Lilly Small?' Finbarr asked.

'Of course not! I sign them Olga Olsen. Oh!' She put her hand across her mouth and said 'I shouldn't have said that. That was a joke. Ha, ha.'

'Ms Small. Do you live here?' Finbarr felt they had wasted enough time.

'Yes. I live here. I live here dangerously. Where do you live?'

'Do you know a Daniel Farrelly?' He considered her question impertinent and ignored it.

'No. Is he nice?' She was now sprawled on the sofa, her drink on the floor within easy reach. She stretched sensually.

'He is a missing person and we wanted to interview Ms Olsen about him.'

'Well you can't.'

'We can't! Why not?'

'Because she's a missing person herself and you can't interview a missing person about another missing person. In fact, come to think of it, you can't interview a missing person about a non-missing person or anything else.'

Finbarr's fourteen-year-old daughter was appearing in the annual play in school and he was supposed to attend it that evening. When he was leaving in the morning his wife had reminded him of it. As he drove in he told himself that he would prefer to be anywhere else in the world except at that play. Now he would have gladly gone to a rake of plays if it would mean getting away from this house on Leeson Park.

'I don't think Ms Olsen is a missing person any longer,' said Aideen who was standing at the window. 'A car has just pulled in and there's a woman getting out of it.'

'She'll punish me! Yes she will!' Lilly had jumped up from the sofa and was now putting her glass back behind the de Sade. 'She doesn't like me to drink without her.'

They heard the hall door open and close and they waited. Lilly was now sitting demurely at the very end of the sofa. Then they heard:

'Lilly. Where are you? I've seen what you did!'

Then the door opened and in came a large woman in a multi-coloured kaftan, and carrying a shopping bag. She wore her grey hair combed straight back in a bun and she had enormous orange earrings and sandals. She had an intense face that bore the marks of much experience as she looked from Lilly to the Gardaí and back again to Lilly.

'Why did you call the Guards?' and without waiting for Lilly's answer went on 'To open the bathroom door for you but as usual they were too late. How long did it take them to travel the five minutes up from Donnybrook? It's disgraceful. A waste of taxpayers' money. I'll be writing …'

'Hold on there,' said Finbarr who wished there was a sane person in the house he could talk to. 'I think there's a small piece of a misunderstanding. I'm Garda Sergeant Walsh and this is Garda O'Neill and you see we weren't <u>called</u> to come here, we came here ourselves as part of an investigation into a missing person. Are you Ms Olsen?'

'Yes Olga Olsen. Why?'

'Do you know Daniel Farrelly?'

'Never heard of him.'

'Did you order a taxi to come here at midday last Tuesday and bring you to Stillorgan?'

'I did indeed.'

'Well we have reason to believe that the driver of that taxi was Daniel Farrelly and he hasn't been seen since.'

'Oh you mean Danny the taxi man. Certainly we know him. Don't we Little Lilly. You remember Danny don't you?'

'Yes. Danny the taxi man was nicer than Paddy the plumber.'

Finbarr looked at Olga Olsen and saw that she had become completely relaxed now and with a smile said 'Let's have a drink in honour of good old Danny. I'll have a g and t, Lilly.' She bent down to get the shopping bag and the neck of the kaftan fell forward so Finbarr could see she wasn't wearing a bra. Lilly giggled and when he looked at her he found she had been looking at him looking down the front of Olga's kaftan. Little Lilly gave him an outrageous wink. He glanced at Garda O'Neill but she was writing something in her notebook and hadn't noticed anything.

'The tonic is in there,' said Olga as she handed the shopping bag to Lilly, 'and so are the condoms. I couldn't get our usual ones so I hope these are O.K.'

'I hope they are too.' Lilly took a packet of condoms out of the bag and started to examine them. 'There's rain forecast for later today. Hey these are the ones Danny said we should get. Goody!'

Olga looked at Finbarr. He was gazing intently at the carpet as if he might find some clue to Daniel Farrelly's whereabouts. Aideen was examining the ceiling possibly for the same reason.

'They're only for the cats,' Olga announced reassuringly. 'Condoms make excellent galoshes for cats.'

'Bet you never heard of ladies putting condoms on their pussies before,' interjected Little Lilly.

Finbarr wondered if Olga Olsen was from Norway or some other Scandinavian country. Her name certainly suggested it but her accent did not. She spoke with the ordinary Dublin accent Finbarr had learned to get used to over the years. Perhaps she had lived here so long she had lost her Norwegian accent or perhaps she had been plain Olga O'Kelly and she had married someone called Olsen. There was no wedding ring to be seen and when she was handing Little Lilly the shopping bag he had looked but had found no mark to suggest she had once worn a wedding ring.

On his eighteenth birthday, after he had made his mind up to become a Garda, his parents had given him a complete set of Arthur Conan Doyle's Sherlock Holmes stories. He had read them enthusiastically thinking that the Holmes technique might become useful to him when he became a sleuth. He had been sadly disappointed.

'Getting back to Daniel Farrelly,' said Finbarr, hoping there would be no more distractions, 'Did he arrive at noon as arranged?'

'Oh yes, twelve noon on the dot. However we weren't quite ready to leave so we asked him in for a drink.' She took the drink Lilly handed to her, drained it in one gulp and handed back the glass for a refill.

'So what time did you leave for Stillorgan at?'

'Oh let me see, it must have been around seven o'clock. Would that be right do you think Lilly?'

'I don't remember I'm afraid.'

'Do you mean to tell me,' Finbarr said, 'that you were here from twelve till seven drinking. The two of you and the taxi man. Did you not have anything to eat?'

'Of course we had something to eat,' Olga was indignant. 'You'd get very drunk if you didn't eat. Drinking on an empty tummy is bad news.' She waved her empty glass at Lilly who said 'Yes we had lovely peanuts. Roasted they were and at the end I had a drop of milk in my brandy. Milk is very good for you.'

'You must all have been very intoxicated by the time you left.'

'We were not intoxicated at all,' said Olga, 'but poor Danny was mouldy drunk. When he came in first he was very quiet and shy. I think Lilly frightened him by telling him she wouldn't pee in his taxi. I think that made him think she might. I've noticed before taxi men are very particular about you peeing in their taxis. They prefer if you get out.

'I think he came from a very deprived background because I made Harvey Wallbangers for us and, do you know, I don't think he'd ever even heard of them before in his life. He liked them though and after the first couple he became more relaxed and sociable.'

'He was a nice man,' observed Lilly as she handed Olga another gin and tonic. 'He had a wonderful singing voice. Sang just like Sinead O'Connor.'

'Tom Jones! It was Tom Jones he sang like, Sweety. You weren't paying attention.'

'No I suppose I wasn't. I was thinking about Stillorgan.'

'Where exactly were you going to in Stillorgan?' asked Finbarr.

'John of Gods of course! What else is there in Stillorgan?'

'What's John of Gods?' Aideen whispered to Finbarr.

'It's where they send people who drink too much so they'll be cured.'

'You see,' Olga continued, 'I decided on Wednesday that Little Lilly had a drink problem and we discussed it and we decided the best thing for her would be to go out to John of Gods for a spell. Isn't that right sweety? That's why I ordered the taxi.'

'Did the taxi man drive you out to Stillorgan at seven in an intoxicated condition?'

'No. No he didn't. Sure he was transmogrified at that stage. We managed to carry him down the steps and Lilly stayed with him while I cut through the church grounds onto the main road where I flagged down a taxi. I got him to come around here to collect the others and off we went.'

'So where did you drop Daniel Farrelly off?'

'John of Gods of course. You see he was so drunk and when Little Lilly promised me she would cut down and not drink Bloody Marys in the morning I felt sorry for her and decided we'd put that Danny fellow in instead.'

Although he didn't know anything about Farrelly's form Finbarr could imagine how relieved he must have felt in John of Gods after spending seven hours in this lunatic asylum.

'So the taxi driver is out in Stillorgan but where is the taxi?'

'It's over there.' Olga went over to the window and pointed at the church. 'The next morning I took the thingamajig off the roof and drove it over to the car park in the church. It's quite safe there.'

'Well thank you, Ms Olsen. You and Ms Small have been very helpful. We won't take up any more of your time right now.'

'Have a drink before you go,' shouted Lilly who skipped around them as if to block their escape route. 'You've done your duty now and Olga will make us all Harvey Wallbangers.' Her lipstick was smudged and her hair was untidy. Perhaps she is forty-five or even fifty, Finbarr thought.

'No, no. Thank you all the same.'

Olga held the hall door open and as they went down the steps they could hear Little Lilly crying out to her.

'Don't beat me, Olga, don't beat me, I promise I'll never pee on the carpet again. Honest.'

Imaginary Friend for Hire

Paul Bassett Davies

This job has always been tough. But in the old days, it was all about magic: the bond between a kid and his Imaginary Friend was sacred. Now, it's all performance targets, customer service, enhancing value – soulless crap. And the brutal rejection. What's wrong with these people? They turn on you at the drop of a hat, or, in this case, a child from out of a tree. But what's the kid thinking of in the first place, with a stunt like that? I blame the special effects they see in all these films. In the old days, a kid knew, deep down, that his Imaginary Friend isn't suddenly going to materialize, like some computer-generated superhero, just because the kid launches himself off a branch, thirty-two feet high (yes, I measured it) and shouts out, "Catch me, Stoffard!" (search me – the names they think up are always weird). No, the bottom line has always been: you want to jump out of a tree, pal, you're on your own. And now the kid's saying I made him do it. "Stoffard told me to." And, of course, the parents believe the lying little turd. Whatever happened to loyalty? And do I get a chance to tell my side of the story? If you think the expression 'non-person' only refers to some loser who was airbrushed out of a 1953 politburo snapshot, think again. I'm living the nightmare. They tell the kid, "Forget about Stoffard," and that's it. I'm history.

Bus

Kath McKay

When Reginald Muponda first started driving the 44C bus, from town to an outer suburb that nobody ever really wanted to go to, he was delighted because everyone called him 'Love'. He'd seen the sign for The Promised Land on the train from London and he thought he'd arrived in heaven. Everybody loved him here. London didn't really agree with him.

'Your hands are your brothers and sisters now,' his mother said when he left his country.

'They will get you out of trouble.' But the only place in London his hands had got him were the inside of washing up bowls and giant dishwashers in big cafés where there was always a smell of grease and everyone spoke a variety of English different to what he'd learnt at school. He learnt to say 'With chips? Double or single? With salad or without?' He wanted to learn computers, but the twelve-hour shifts in the café meant he was fit only for bed by the evening.

So when he saw the advert – 'Bus drivers wanted – Move north to a better life,' he applied. Delighted to be accepted, he embarked on the training course with enthusiasm. He could already drive, and potholes back home were so much more spectacular than here – deep caves where buses disappeared and lakes formed. Even though people here moaned about traffic he thought it was nothing. Traffic he could cope with. Traffic was just your terrain, something to get through each day, and he liked the way sometimes you had to be relaxed and philosophical, idling your engine, and other times (rarer, he admitted) you could zip along in the bus lane, powering the beast on, believing you were going somewhere, you had a purpose.

He passed the test with the highest grade and was given his own route. 44C, the path to heaven.

He smiled at people, collected their fare. He got to know the regulars. Even the occasional 'You with your big fat nigger legs sitting there,' didn't put him off. He smiled at the racists and other people around tutted and said 'There's no need for that,' moving away from the disapproved ones. Reginald muttered under his breath 'Forgive them lord, for they know not what they do.'

His patience and forbearance seemed to infuriate some people and once one man even went to raise his hand. This man was smartly dressed, in a suit, with a mean, squirrelly face. But someone else grabbed the man's hand and told him to sling his hook. Reginald hadn't heard that expression before, but he noted it down in the little vocabulary book he filled in each night. He was learning such interesting words. Carney, whilst, ginnel, boxty. Each night he'd practise. I want to say bus, he said to the mirror. It came out as bas.

He got to know those who went shopping in town, the pensioners, the twirlies who got on before the cheap fares started and tried holding up the bus until the deadline passed. It was a game with them.

'I tell you,' he'd say, smiling like them.

'Get on, and I will take your fare in a minute.'

He met the men who signed on, the schoolkids, the late night cleaners and the care assistants from the big care homes in the suburbs. For a long time he was happy. No matter that his single room was dark and there was a strange smell from the drains, at least he had a room. Sometimes, just as he arrived at his door, he thought for a second his wife and daughter might be there, like on that day back home he'd arrived from work as usual. There were signs of struggle – a table overturned, the bedclothes ruffled, dishes smashed. Now there was just a dripping tap and the loud tick tock of the alarm clock. He cooked great bowls of rice and meat and walked in the park on Sunday and shopped at the local supermarket where the security guard was an African from back home who spoke to him in Ndebele. He found out where to buy toilet rolls cheap, and oranges. He borrowed library books and tapes. But something was missing.

So he started to decorate the bus. He found piles of newspapers near the recycling bins, and each morning carried them onto his bus, cut them into strips, wet them with bottles of water, and laid them on the floor of the bus, covering every surface up to the back. He wanted no surface left uncovered. Every evening the bus went into the garage like this and each morning it came out clean. Somebody must have cleared it, but nobody ever said anything. Each day Reginald collected newspapers, wet them, cut them into strips, and laid them on the floor. Some mornings he noticed the look of surprise in the passengers' eyes, but nobody complained. He figured that if he covered every surface, things would work out. At night, restless, he dreamt of his wife and daughter. Each morning he fingered their bracelets, the only things he had left.

After a week of decorating the bus, one of those kindly older ladies who reminded him of the grandmothers back in his village asked 'How are you?' after she'd paid her fare.

'Not so bad,' he said, feeling the tears welling up. Outside, the rain had started. The sky was grey and overcast. He shivered. She touched his arm, turned round and whistled to her friends. As the bus moved on towards town they began to clear it up. They scooted up and down, gathering papers, and stuffed them into plastic bags.

'Time,' she grinned, as she got off the bus with her friends, carrying the bags with them.

'Our job, that's what we do.'

And the bus was clean and new again, a proud bus, its engine roaring.

'Thank you,' he shouted after her.

'No problem' she said.

It was as if she'd known something, for the next stop an inspector got on. This inspector was an affable man, always making conversation. Reginald hadn't seen the inspector all the previous week. The man told him he'd had the flu.

'You're doing well. Bus nice and clean.'

Reginald grunted.

'Probably a bit cold and wet for you.'

'I come from the mountains.'

'Oh, do they have mountains there?'

Reginald smiled. Not worth getting upset. The inspector wasn't aggressive, just ignorant. He didn't mean any harm, not like that woman who threw a banana once. She'd aimed to hit him. It had taken Reginald a while to realise you didn't really have to answer the inspector. He figured that the Inspector was a little deaf.

The Inspector got off at the terminus where Reginald went for his break. Reginald knew he'd been lucky, but the next day he found himself again carrying the newspapers onto the bus, cutting them into strips, wetting them, decorating the bus. The kindly woman cleared up the bus again, with her friends.

The third day, Wednesday, he collected the newspapers, cut them into strips, wet them and decorated the bus. This third day the kindly lady did not get on and as he approached the town, knowing the Inspector would almost certainly appear, Reginald began to feel tense. The bus was full of schoolkids carrying bags and rolled up free newspapers. They were especially loud today. For the first time it struck him that what he was doing would be seen as wrong and he could lose his job. A girl got off the bus, finished a can of coke, and threw the can on the pavement. Reginald noticed the rubbish in the streets, the chip wrappers, the burger cartons. Maybe he would be seen as a bad example to the kids. Reginald began to sweat.

Suddenly, at a little used stop, the tiniest woman in the world, with a headdress like a nun's, showed her pass and got on. Hunchbacked, as she walked she sloped a little to the left, and as she went past she turned towards him so that his arm brushed her hump, as solid and muscular as a wing. Back home hunchbacks were lucky.

She fixed her eyes on the floor.

'Disgraceful,' she said, addressing the bus passengers.

'This man needs help. It's up to us.'

'Get to work,' she ordered, and the passengers rose as one, stuffing the paper into bags, which they deposited neatly by the door. Schoolkids even rubbed at the windows, which had built up layers of dust, marvelling at the world outside, exclaiming at birds and trees, blue sky, bright light.

'See, it looks better, dunnit,' said one of them to Reginald.

'Boss,' said another. Reginald nodded.

And so he drove along with the windows clean and the bus clean and the kids had sensible discussions about what they wanted to be when they grew up and he heard one girl say 'I wanna be a bus driver cos you can help people,' and Reginald felt his chest swelling like it hadn't swelled since the day his daughter took her first step. He brushed the tears away.

The hunchbacked lady rang the bell near the hospital stop.

'Going to see my husband,' she said, handing him a card with a number on it.

'You'll be all right now.' He looked at the card.

'Any problem solved,' it said.

'Debt. Marital problems. Landlord difficulties. Homesickness. Bothering by evil spirits. He can unite your family. He will make you success in life. Trouble with the police. Regarding any of your human difficulties. Guaranteed results. Also impotency problems. Quick, fast, efficient.' And she tripped off, with her left-leaning gait, walking past the hospital, towards the cemetery.

On his day off on Saturday he went to see the man listed on the card. The man listened to his story for a long time, leaning back, with his eyes closed. At one point Reginald thought the man was asleep, but then his eyelids flickered. When Reginald finished, the man went to a cupboard and brought out a small bag filled with soil.

'This is soil from your homeland,' he said.

'You need to plant something in it.'

Reginald snorted. How could it be soil from his homeland? He hadn't even told the man where he was from. It was probably from B & Q. But he bought a swelling bulb anyway on the way home and transferred the bulb from its flimsy container into a bigger bowl with the soil. Over the next few weeks he watched the bulb fatten and burst into glorious yellow.

The day the bulb came into full flower, the old hunchbacked woman came to him in a dream. In the dream they were up in the mountains back home and she spoke to him in Ndebele. She gestured and pointed upwards, and when he looked up, high on a rise in the mountains, there were two body-shaped humps, the graves of his daughter and wife, and the graves were piled up with flowers, yellow flowers covering every last surface so that you could hardly see the bumps. Down below a deep lake reflected the mass of yellow flowers.

When he woke, he knew the dream couldn't be true. They had never found the bodies, and probably never would.

But something had shifted in him and he decided to go for a swim that night after work. He'd been meaning to go all year. The local library was just next to the pool. On a whim, he enrolled in an Introduction to the Internet course.

In the deep end of the pool there was a girl in a blue costume who reminded him of his wife when younger. He took a deep breath, lifted his right arm, stretched over the surface of the water, kicked.

Skin Song

Mary Leland

'Begin to breathe a little bit sooner – it's *legato*, don't allow it to become too agitated. Smooth, smooth, the long long breath. Again!'

Again. The voice sang out. Not full, there was no need for that. The woman stood away from the piano, away from it across the bare boards of the room, her face in the striped shadow cast by the sunlight through the louvres.

Here were the picture and the sound coming together for Geraldine; her mother apart yet embodying the events of the room. At the piano a man, his back to Geraldine who was – where?

There had been a little *pouffe* made in triangles of coloured leather. In what room or in which town it had been there for Geraldine to sit on she was never to remember although the triangles still held their cracked leathery shape in her mind.

The *pouffe* was in this picture which surely was of those days in which Beata sang to keep at work, when her voice was in training, when it was strong, committed to its life.

It had been summer, for Geraldine was not at school. Perhaps in the last years of Beata's last love, or of its equally abrasive, equally destructive facsimile. At a time when that condition, or its simulation, had begun its infiltration, its colonisation of Beata's being so that her need of it banished other needs. As it banished Geraldine, her daughter.

Summer, and Geraldine not a small child despite the little *pouffe*. Then: whose was that other voice, whose hand on the piano?

'Make a little more space around it. You must visualise the shape of the sound, round it, make it longer as you ascend, getting the line and singing all through the line. Again!'

Again the notes ascended. Geraldine heard the obedient voice re-direct itself and flow into its instructions. As the key came from the piano, holding the sound until the voice struck, the girl wondered at the skilled adjustment: how the voice could stop and then, having listened to something other than itself, take off with no cough, no fractious breath to intervene as the melody floated seamless on the air.

When the man spoke Beata looked at him. When his fingers touched the keys she looked away across the room to the layered glow on the floorboards. The song would come again as if it had not been interrupted. Sometimes Beata would shift the stance of her feet on the floor, shifting to get purchase, clutching the floor with her feet as if to lever a stronger, more resonant tone from the drum of her sternum.

'Don't worry about the breath. Good singers breathe all over the place, you're thinking too much about the breath. Wait – let me show you.'

He got up. Grey-haired, yes, a beard of mixed black and grey and white hairs, not long, close to his chin but sharp-cut, defined as a mannerism. He wore a shirt, was it blue? There was something blue, a tie, not a tie but a scarf, a jabot or cravat, that was blue, and the shirt was white, loose-sleeved with the cuffs open, pushed back to show skin pelted with hair.

As he stood behind her mother Geraldine recognised him as tall: tall, bearded, coaching Beata in a list of songs, the French songs she said – to please him? – she insisted she loved; she had not then realised what a challenge that music would be for her, what it would reveal about her technique, which was not subtle. Well then: more need, more time, for this teaching.

Arnaud: Geraldine never in his hearing gave him that name. It was a detail of the dream memory of a half-spent adolescence. In Arnaud, Geraldine revived M. Martellet. 'Arnaud,' Beata's whisper was a slur in her voice, a velvet rasp as the thin bone of her jaw grazed itself on his hand. Geraldine had seen animals make a gesture, a fluid sideways scratching motion of exactly similar grace.

Beata's neck arched against his hand where he had placed it to press the fluid chords of her throat. She brought her hand to cover his pressure beneath her breast-bone, beneath her breasts. Geraldine saw her mother's white fingers spread, flexing as the man pushed the heel of his palm against her body. 'Arnaud,' Beata said, the word thick as if slow to leave her lips. Weighted with satin hair her head turned inwards to his face, lifting up to the scratch of his beard, not languid despite the laboured word.

There was silence, the silence of breathing and deliberation. Geraldine saw the smile separate beard and moustache, saw her mother's answering smile, saw her mother's eyes closing in a long sigh as Martellet's mouth, so wetly pink beneath the hair, fastened on the skin of the stretched neck.

Something separated them. Had Geraldine stirred? Even in parting they were graceful, guiltless. Had Geraldine stirred, stung by a sense within herself of what hung between them, not the music merely?

'This is *bel canto.*' Martellet instructed the submissive Beata. 'This is demanding. Only if you have the good *bel canto* style should you attempt French song. You must have the technique so secure that it is possible to forget about it, to know that the breath will sustain the line without even thinking, so smooth it must be, unthinkable that it might fail you. So – let the syllables flow, sing on right through the line, sing on!'

That was singing. This is singing, Geraldine had told herself, phrases forming around the words within her consciousness. Beata's voice rang on, realising what Martellet had told her; it was the easiest thing in the world, this singing, if everything were right. Easy because it was natural. The natural way to sing. A French melody for an English song.

Now sleeps the crimson petal now the white.

Syllables clung to the line of melody like birds resting on a branch: settled, balanced, yet ready for flight. Geraldine heard them in her own song: The firefly wakens, waken thou with me. The song was an echo. The voice from which the echo sprang was that of Martellet, leading Geraldine through the verses, his palm at her vibrating throat.

There was a chronology of recall; in the time-scale of her life Geraldine was never to be certain of the year, the month, the hour of this over-heard, over-witnessed lesson, of where it came in the calendar of consciousness. It seemed to be a precedence, an overture rather than an intermezzo. Or a prologue to a story whose epilogue was Geraldine's own entire adult life, beginning – where?

That house in Italy. On the sea, beside a lake, where had it been with its sheen of water washed on walls of rooms previously unknown to Geraldine? He had been there – Martellet. It was her first recollection of the beard. Arnaud, arrived to meet Beata, who was absent.

Some laughter about it, about her mother, produced in the waiting Geraldine a defensive boldness. It made her say to the woman she understood to be her hostess – a princess of splendid title wearing diamonds, like *applique,* in daytime – that she did not wish to be with people who derided her parent. The princess patted her cheek and said that Beata was surely glad to have so loyal a child. Geraldine knew this to be unlikely but was appeased by a promise of company while she waited: she would not be lonely, the princess said. Her own nieces and nephews were visiting from Berlin. They would take her to swim, to ride in the hills; they would make music together. Geraldine would not be lonely.

The nephews were darkly Italianate, the girls sultry blondes impatient with quartets and preferring violent tennis. The rides to the hills were too ambitious for Geraldine, embarrassed by having to borrow breeches in order to mount astride ... Absorbed by the swimming, the riding, the tennis, the two nieces were no difficulty for the hospitable princess. More indolent, the boys swam lazily, calling to Geraldine as they thrust their heads out of the water, diving sleek as seals between their calls.

An almost out-grown swimsuit made her self-conscious but at length she joined them, the water funnelling and closing in a blue iridescent sheet over her face as she fell, then lifting her up again, soaring, to find Paolo and Stefano grinning at her with wide glistening mouths.

Was it salt? Was it lake water, could it have been Como – she had been there once certainly, was that where the white villa was with its balcony and flowers? But there had been no Stefano there, no blond girls cycling morning after morning to the farm where horses were kept for their entertainment. Yet that day's plunge and that surge back to the sparkle of light and friendliness, wherever it had been, had been the prelude to Martellet. Wherever it had been, he was already in the house when Geraldine arrived, waiting, like her, for Beata.

Geraldine had come alone. At I5 she was an accomplished traveller.

She saw the bearded man among the guests but the beard was all that distinguished him and even though she quickly understood that he too expected Beata to arrive before them both, to be there in fact to welcome him for she was the motive of his visit – even as she quickly grasped all this Geraldine had no reason to speak to him. Her knowledge came from other sources, from the air, it seemed sometimes, so easily did explanation, like expectation, diffuse itself among the gathering.

Waiting but not discontented she had put her swimsuit on in her bedroom. After swimming the boys, a few years older than she but still loudly playful, had left to dress in the bathing cabin and Geraldine went on up the terraced steps alone, feeling the heat dry the water from her skin, shaking her hair free of its braid so that the sun could soak the sea from her head. Her lifted arm caught the light shining on the little beads of water which ran almost from her fingers to her shoulder. She shook her arm to watch the droplets shine and scatter and then disappear and she swung her hair loose and around in a suddenly joyous, swerving surge and all its brightness of water flashed and danced around her.

The swimsuit of white puckered cotton was like a child's garment straining against her body, but now it was wet she no longer felt awkward but confident and free-moving and her walk towards the villa was an easy swinging stride. Martellet was up there on the terrace, watching her.

She saw him as she reached him. His white straw hat was peaked at a slant. His shirt was open at the neck, he wore no tie or jacket with his white trousers. He did not get up but as Geraldine came near he raised his hat in a salute which was not mocking but was not entirely serious. Aware of this, and also that she looked young and clean and sure-footed while he sat there in a cane verandah chair, Geraldine acknowledged him with a cool little dip of her head, something she had seen Beata do to men who did not interest her, men with whom she did not have to pretend.

When she had changed Geraldine found Paolo tuning his violin in one of the salons – waiting, he said, for Stefano. The princess had asked them to play to the company this evening and they might do so although of course not without rehearsal. This easy assumption that it was appropriate for the princess to invite their performance before guests whom Geraldine had heard Beata describe as 'august' (but why then was Beata herself missing?) impressed Geraldine immensely. The suggestion that the two boys would play for these people only if it suited them thrilled her, their indifference seemed as daring as their dives. They were so young, little older than herself, what had made them so independent of the approval now at their disposal? What had made them so confident of applause, and so keen that it must be applause worth winning? They seemed to her to have a habit of decision over their own lives.

When Stefano came in he invited Geraldine to stand in the well of the piano. He showed her the music, some English songs, they had been reading them for fun. She began to sing, laughing because her breathing was only a trick learned by listening to Beata, by watching her. And Paolo said – 'No! Do it correctly! Be serious.'

'But I can't,' she protested. 'I'm not a singer. And it's so sad.'

'Do,' he said. And Stefano touched the chords again, opening the song like a languorous magician. 'Do,' said Stefano. 'It will be only fun still, making music like this is not too serious, we enjoy it. Our lives do not depend on it. Sing with us.'

The opening, alluring sounds led her on although she trembled at first. This was not like singing at school. This was a close attention, knowledgeable yet casual, the notes held for her until she made them secure. Then Paolo played, at Stefano's reminder repeating a phrase where the slurs were too distinct. They played together, the two young men, sure of what they were doing, united by its rightness, the fidelity of their unison an aural happiness filling the room, embracing Geraldine.

Even if they had seen Martellet as he halted at the doorway they were so pleased with themselves they would not have recognised him. He might have entered the room – although he did not – without disturbing them. When their music ended he was gone.

Then came dinner on the terrace. Geraldine was invited to change her dress as they did on Sundays in school. Because she had nothing else she put on the flowered crepe frock with slanting shoulders which made sleeves although there were no sleeves to it. It was light, and dove-coloured. Not girlish. She felt like a moth.

On the table the candles were set in bowls of flowers, wicks floating among petals in tiny porcelain basins. The maidservants were smiling but silent as they brought plates and carried them away; the wine glinted bright and dark in the crystal carafes, the food came in little sportive gusts, plentiful, exclaimed over, passed around, tasted, forgotten.

After that the music. Paolo played with Stefano, violin leaning to the keyboard, and then one of their sisters produced her silver flute and Mozart as well as Schubert and Weber thickened like a scent on the warm retentive air. Debussy, and Mahler, a scattering of what to Geraldine were less familiar names. All this music, and no Beata, and the great, seductive charm of it all was the acceptance that this music belonged to these young people; it was as though the adults were the guests at the feast displayed by the young people.

This was a wonder to Geraldine in whose life the only music held to be worth hearing was the property of adults. Here the pair of boys and their two sisters claimed it without challenge, their listeners acquiescing in their possessiveness. Geraldine thought they were proud of it, proud of the promise made here on the terrace as though the performance were more pledge than pleasure. And it seemed that there was a sympathy between them all on that terrace, on that evening, even as the excitement of the music faded with the sun. Gentler airs were heard, there was a murmur of praise for a tenor who sang with tenderness rather than passion. On the sea, on the lake, the light sank down to darkness, and Geraldine was lost in the sway of a consensus unprecedented in all her life before. She felt glowingly conscious that her eyes were bright, her cheeks warm, that she was here without Beata and accepted without her, a part of all that was happening.

Martellet had come to sit close to her. He brought a cushion for himself which he put on the tiles at her feet where he could lean back against the side of her chair. He wore no hat now but his jacket was neat, as if new, white as his trousers, and his shoes, Geraldine saw as he stretched his legs out on the floor, were white also, a soft creamy colour not as pale as his socks. His cravat gleamed like silk, the colours rippling together under the dark jut of his beard. He drew his legs up as if uncomfortable, and his knee touched Geraldine's leg. She shifted delicately so as not to disturb him; delicately, but unmistakably.

Perhaps he did not notice, for he let his hand stray along her unstockinged leg, down towards the instep, a warm friendly stroke down the bone making her shiver. Now she could not move away for to do so would make so marked a movement that it would be noticed by others. And yet there was no purpose in the motion; he did not press or squeeze nor did he seek to stroke above her knee, it was as though she were a cat, her fur amenable to his restless hand.

And she grew drowsy as the night let down its shadows. She had no sense of the time, only of softening light and the wavering murmur of voices. There was nothing to be done until Beata came and told her where they were to go, and with whom. Lulled, she let the distant questions hover. Soon she would leave this place. It was an interlude.

It might be that she would leave without saying farewell to Paolo or Stefano or their sisters. She might never meet any of them again. Arrivals and departures were frequent and sudden in her life.

The hand against her skin had changed. The palm was open now and like a cup on the flesh at the back of her leg, not moving up and down but pressing, gently, a finger on the pulse in the hollow of her knee. She had never known that pulse before, never explored it but now it was familiar and his hand was on that pulse, on the tempo of her body.

Trays of sweetmeats were brought. Lamps were lit in the corners of connecting rooms. Insects glistened and fell. Geraldine saw Stefano looking away abstracted, his profile stencilled against the dusk. He was looking away from the lights and the conversations towards the rim of hills visible by the reflected glow on the water. Could she go to him and say – what could she say that would not break his mood and claim more attention for herself than this troubling hand deserved?

There was Paolo, bringing a plate and a wide shallow glass to a woman who stood near the balcony's rim, a woman with shingled hair, her face animated with an expression Geraldine had seen before, Beata had perfected it, it was meant to engage, not to enthrall. And Paolo was engaged, his own face bright.

Resting his hand on the arm of her chair Martellet got to his feet without once glancing at Geraldine. She saw how he exchanged a look with the princess whose laugh was at his clumsiness in rising from his youthful pose on the ground. Geraldine got up immediately as if released, going behind her chair to skirt the clustered room and find her way outside without interception. A dense blue gloaming cloaked the garden doors, all open to the night. It was a fairy-tale garden, the starry sky held above it by the cypress trees, no cry now from the peacocks roosting on the high courtyard walls. She lingered for a moment to breathe in the scents escaping as if from a phial along the bowered paths.

A noise behind her made her spin back to the light; it was the princess coming to see if there were anything she wanted before going to bed. To see – as Geraldine was to assure herself later, when she needed to know that there had been those who had cared for her, there had been the Princess – to see that she went to bed safely, unafraid, undisturbed.

Upstairs the tiled corridor was cool, the resumed music far away. Geraldine had the sense that up here she was the only waking being, so distant was all else. In the bathroom her unbraided hair still had a trace of dampness. As water filled the bowl and her hands sank to the white marble fount she thought of the words of that song on the piano, that song in the studio: how present it was, the cypress, the meteor's furrow, the milk-white birds. *Bel canto.* 'Now folds the lily all her sweetness up And slips into the bosom of the lake ...'

She hummed slowly as she rinsed her face, seeing the colour come under her skin, her hair curl just there at the edges where it met her forehead, the little screwed-up curls. On the terrace when she had been swimming, coming back up to the terrace and passing him, she had seen Martellet's shirt open on little grey curls, little black curls.

He was waiting for her when she came out of the bathroom. With the shock came certainty. He was there for her. He held out his hand, looking at her with a question in his face, and also with the answer. Would she? Would she?

She put her hand in his.

Waking alone the next morning Geraldine felt as if she were going to have to go through the rest of her life without her skin. Not in pain, but exposed. What had happened had been explicit. 'You are so young,' Martellet had said before he kissed her. 'I saw you singing.' Saw, and Geraldine's mind caught the difference, saw not heard.

It had been astonishing, and a secret she knew must be kept forever. Those red lips on her body. Silky in their slide between her breasts. The rasp of unexpected hair, the words which banished shame and yet made secrecy emphatic. But nothing about it, he had explained with a tenderness she suspected was not addressed to her but to the act itself, nothing about it was unique. It was what was between men and women.

That day Beata soared into the villa, unaccompanied, sweet with effortless apologies, silencing the athletic girls and captivating Paolo and Stefano. She surrendered to the princess armloads of books and flowers and whole catalogues of accurate compliments. She was brightness personified as if she reflected the sun's own radiance. People swarmed about her and she called just once for Geraldine; she exclaimed at Geraldine's height, her maturity, her colour. She was all praise, all fondness. The way she could be.

That observance over Geraldine could disappear again, to enter her new self. Beata had already turned to the lurking Martellet. To Arnaud. There was so much they must discuss; he would not be angry with her for this delay? Their murmurs were a haze in Geraldine's ears. She saw Paolo and Stefano wander towards the water, wading rather than diving, as if reluctant. From the water they could see Beata, her parasol foaming above her wide veiled ribboned flowered hat, a hat by that time a head-dress of a banished era but an opulent fashion which suited Beata and which therefore she would retain. Thus hat and sunshade floated together above the flowers on the terrace, above the sea, above the lake. White froth on paler froth, light as a breath, a sigh.

The boys leapt up through the ripples, performing like young dolphins although if they could see the cloud of lace and blossoms then they must also see Martellet, his hat tipped a little to one side. Yet they thrust themselves through the water, the young dolphins, performing not with lyre and chord but with skin and sinew and smooth sheaves of hair.

Watching from the sill of her window Geraldine knew she would never see them again as they were then, as she was then. Never again would she stand with Stefano's hand at her waist, his other hand punctuating a measure in the air, timing the cadence for her voice. She looked down towards the swimmers: she glanced over the terrace, over the tiered confection of delicate pastel tissue that was Beata, over Martellet with his cravat a dashing twist of scarlet, his hands lightly sifting the barred pages in his lap. Hearing the shouts of the boys in the water Geraldine felt something hard and wild and shocking flare through her rib-cage.

It was only anger, and loss, but the intensity was new to her, she thought. Rage spurted in tears, she felt the heat, the wetness, on her face. Rage as she had seen it in Beata, a bitter surge which made her clutch at her chest as if to hold it in, to hold it back for fear it might, it must, burst through her skin, shredding like parchment.

This rage was aimless. It had no focus for all its force. Its source was a misery which was never to be so acute again although of course she could not know that. She thought this was to be her private curse. It took hold of her and she shook at her perch on the window-ledge so that she drew back into the cooler shadows of the room, denying to herself the brightness, the challenging laughter of the boys, the collusion on the terrace.

Her adult life was born at this window over the terrace, the steps, the broad terrazo floors with their burden of voices, the luminous water with its shouting, jumping, glorious young men. Wherever it had been. Whenever it had been.

'Arnaud,' Beata's caressing whisper came again. On the studio wall the light waited in empty staves. The man's hand soothed the taut, turned neck, his head bent to let his mouth, so red within the beard, hiss beneath her ear, absorbed. They were not disturbed by Geraldine sitting somewhere beyond them, not between. They came apart on his murmur: 'A little too much *vibrato,* my darling. We will deal with it later.' As he walked back to the piano Geraldine, unmoving, felt her throat tighten. She knew herself to be invisible to them both, although she sat there without her skin.

Winner of the Fish Short Story Prize **Marc Phillips**

lives in Texas. He's been writing fiction for almost three years, and his poetry and non-fiction have appeared in print since 1991. 'The Mountains of Mars' is his first short story published abroad, and promises to generate considerably less flak for the author than most of his others. He welcomes comments on all his work, and can be contacted at rms2@att.net.

Second in the Fish Short Story Prize **Jo Campbell**

always wanted to write but reading English at university convinced her that she had nothing worthwhile to contribute to the canon of English literature, so she became a civil servant instead. Forty years later, post-retirement, she thought damn it, let's have a go anyway, and has now been writing short stories for about five years. Her work was first published in the Asham Award anthology for '02. Jo is married with two grown-up children and lives in London.

Third in the Fish Short Story Prize **Barry Troy**

An Irish engineer, he has worked in Europe, the Middle East and Asia. He has had one novel published - *Dirty Money*. Another novel is currently under consideration for publication. His short story 'Rain' was included in the *Fish Anthology 2004*. He is currently working on a new novel and several short stories.

Joint Winner of the Fish One Page Story Prize **Tom Murray**

lives in the Scottish Borders. He has had a number of plays for both young people and adults performed at various venues including the Traverse Theatre, Edinburgh and the Arches Theatre, Glasgow. His stories and poems have been widely published in literary magazines in the UK, and in the USA and Canada. He is co-editor of the Eildon Tree Magazine.

Caroline Koeppel

A native New Yorker, Caroline's stories have been published in several commercial and literary magazines. 'How to Kill a Latin Teacher' was inspired by six years of Latin in an all girls' school culminating in a class trip to Italy with the bluest of blue-haired Latin teachers. A graduate of the MFA program at Columbia University, Caroline now teaches writing at Hunter College in New York City.

Joint Winner of the Fish One Page Story Prize

Brian Tiernan

was born Dublin 1939 - next day Hitler invaded Poland.
Brought up in the Irish midlands - geographical, the dead centre of Ireland was the outside lav in Brian's back yard.
Jobs in Dublin and London included bacon inspector - warble fly inspector - insurance salesman - shipping clerk - local government - building game - tip boss - hoover salesman - bookmaker - tipster - professional gambler.
Now semi-retired living in Covent Garden.

Editor's Choice

Selma Dabbagh

is an Anglo-Palestinian writer who is sometimes also a lawyer. Educated in England and Kuwait, she previously worked with human rights organisations in Jerusalem, Cairo and London. She went on to work as a Legal Aid lawyer in South London until she moved to Bahrain with her husband's work in 2000. Selma gave up a position as in-house counsel in May 2004 in order to write. She was a finalist in last year's Fish Short Story Competition with her first story, 'Aubergine'. This year she was short listed for the 2005 Raymond Carver Award and her story 'Down the Market' was adopted by English PEN as their submission to International PEN's David TK Wong Short Story Prize 2005. Next year, her work is to appear in *Arab-American and Anglo-Arab Writers* (ed. N Handal), Interlink (forthcoming March 2006). She is really into her first novel at the moment.

Jessica Wells

works as a spy for The Juilliard School in New York City. She has lived in uptown Manhattan for the past nine years. She graduated from Barnard College with a degree in Creative Writing, and is a founding member of the Breadbasket Writing Group. In 2004, she and her boyfriend published a deck of anti-Bush playing cards called "Freedom Cards," which are available at www.seanboggs.com. An accomplished quilter, Ms. Wells also enjoys travelling, knitting, learning German, drawing maps, and rearing hamsters.

Paul Bassett Davies

wrote the screenplay for the feature animation film *The Magic Roundabout* and is currently writing the screenplay for a film starring 1960s counterculture heroes, *The Fabulous Furry Freak Brothers.* He founded the Crystal Theatre, acclaimed for pioneering multimedia work in the 1970s and 80s. Two of his one-man shows were Perrier Award finalists at the Edinburgh Festival. He was the vocalist in punk band *Shoes For Industry.*

He has written and directed stage productions, short films and music videos, and has been a radio producer.

He has also worked as a minicab driver, a gardener, and a DJ in a strip club. He is a ventriloquist with his own doll (Sailor Boy).

Rebecca Smith

is a 21-year-old student from a village in West Yorkshire. She studies business economics and finance at Loughborough University, but has spent the last nine months at Carol III University in Madrid studying economics and learning Spanish.

She has been writing short quirky stories since she was a child. The eccentricity gene that runs through her mother's family has turned out to be a blessing when creating these pieces.

This is the first competition she has entered and she is thrilled to have 'The Butterfly Slippers' published.

Rob Pateman

Born in Romford, Essex, Rob Pateman lives in Kennington, London. Happy, lanky and a liability on in-line skates, Rob is looking for an outlet for his first novel and getting into a second. Unfortunately his tennis ability is more Shirley Williams than Venus Williams but, as with his writing, he's working on it.

Anthony M. O'Sullivan

American-Irish, ex-merchant seaman, copywriter and ad agency creative director. Left advertising to write fiction. Married, lives in Howth with four daughters and six grandchildren within cannon shot. Writes a little, sails a lot.

Hugo Kelly

genuine, trustworthy writer and librarian in his late thirties. WLTM kind, generous publisher to share good times and perhaps lead to serious relationship. Likes drinking late and solving extraordinarily complex geopolitical situations with profound yet simple insights. Previous stories have appeared in the *Sunday Tribune*, the *Fish Anthology 1999, Cúirt Annual, Books Ireland* amongst other publications. Currently working on a novel for children. Only sincere responses please. GSOH essential.

Tessa Green

splits her time between the North East of England and Greece and between law and painting. She has recently taken up writing and this short short story is the first piece she's had published.

Susi Klare

was born in Vienna, Austria, but is now deeply rooted in the American West. She is the recipient of a 2001 Oregon Literary Arts Fellowship and numerous literary prizes. Her stories have been published in *Peregrine, Other Voices, Carve Magazine, River City,* and are pending publication in *Dogwood* and *Mississippi Review.* Her recently completed book is entitled *Stories from the Middle of Nowhere.*

Richard Dunford

Richard's writing career currently consists of a huge collection of rejection letters from magazines, agents and publishers most of which saying "its a little too different for us".
He is also 33.3% of the unsigned but will probably be signed any day (please god) indie/alternative rock band *Brandy Alexander.* Check out www.brandyalexander.co.uk

Jennifer A. Donnelly

is American, but has been living in Paris for six years. She has done work for academic and business publications, political editorialists and art historians, cultural ambassadors and corporations, and is completing a doctorate on art museums. She is currently writing a collection of stories, of which 'The Object of Desire', her first published piece of fiction, is one.

Clare S. Birchall

by day, is a university lecturer, teaching young adults things they may or may not need to know, and publishing academic books on topics of marginal interest. By night, she is a writer of fiction. Like clubbers who forget their shades or vampires in search of dessert, she sometimes wishes the sun wouldn't rise for another couple of hours. She lives in London with a half-finished novel and a monkey.

Tomás O'Beirne

is a Dublin-born architect who began writing short stories because planning permission is not required for that activity.
So far he has had a story, 'The Tangerine Towel', published in *Whispers and Shouts*, a piece in the *Sunday Miscellany Anthology*, and numerous letters to Madam in the *Irish Times.*
He lives in Dublin 4, but has travelled extensively in Dublin 1, 2 and 6.

Kath McKay

was born in Liverpool, studied in Belfast and London and lives in Leeds. Published a novel *Waiting for the Morning,* The Women's Press 1991, and a collection of poetry, *Anyone Left Standing,* The Poetry Business, 1998.
After working in journalism, she started teaching creative writing to adults in 1987, but has cut back after gaining a 2004 Arts Council of England Writers' Award for short stories. She is working with Finnish writers on Interland (www.intland.net). She mentors on the Crossing Borders scheme for African writers (www.crossingborders-africanwriting.org). She is collaborating on a project about teeth with a visual artist, Janis Goodman. They previously produced a *Little Book of Lice* (Yorkshire Arts 1998).

Mary Leland

is a freelance journalist living in Cork city. She writes for *The Irish Examiner, The Irish Times* and *The Sunday Independent* and is the author of two novels *The Killeen* (London 1985, New York 1986) and *Approaching Priests* (London 1991) as well as a collection of short stories *The Little Galloway Girls* (London 1986). Her fiction has been broadcast in Ireland and the UK and is continually included in anthologies. Cork University Press published *The Lie of the Land; Journeys through Literary Cork* in 1999 and the Cork Harbour Board published *That Endless Adventure; a History of the Cork Harbour Commissioners* in 2001.

Authors Who Reached the Final Short List

in the Short Story Prize

Kristina Amadeus

Rebecca Bryant

Jo Campbell

Fleur Chapman

Ronald Currie, Jr.

Stephen Cusack

Paul Bassett Davies

Michael Donnellan

Jennifer A. Donnelly

Rebecca Graham

John Hall

Thomas J. Harrison

Eli Hastings

Bonnie Hearn Hill

Kunthavai Jayadevan

Rosemary Jenkinson

Hugo Kelly

Susi Klare

Caroline Koeppel

Dyland Landis

Tom Lee

Mary Leland

Sean Lusk

Bonnie McCune

Kath McKay

Ian Madden

Linda Mannheim

Tomás O'Beirne

Elizabeth Oness

Paddy O'Reilly

Marc Phillips

Ian Seed

Jane Sellers

Lynn M. Stegner

M.M. Stockman

Marianne Taylor

Barry Troy

John Welch

John Wheway

Tobias Williams

Beth Williamson

Authors Who Reached the Final Short List in the One Page Story Prize

Clare S. Birchall
Tim Booth
David Brookes
Jenny R. Browder
J.A. Brown
Stephen Brown
Sally Coelho
Paul Cuddihy
Paul Bassett Davies
Richard Dunford
Jonathan Evison
Tim Foley
Frances Garrood
Tessa Green
Justin Andrew Hudnall
Nicola Jennings
J.R. Johnson
Stephen Kennedy
Mal King

Marie MacSweeney
Robert McLoughlin
Maggie Mealy
Eoin Mulvihill
Tom Murray
Anthony M. O'Sullivan
David O'Sullivan
Mark O'Toole
Rob Pateman
Mary Rodenhurst
Maureen A. Sherbondy
Pauline Mary Smith
Rebecca Smith
Michael Takemoto
Brian Tiernan
J. Tomasz
Nicolas Tucker
Colin Upton
Jessica Wells

Authors Who Reached the Initial Short List in the Fish Short Story Prize

Kristina Amadeus, Tejaswini Apte, Maureen Bartlett, Judith Batalion, Jeremy Baumann, Lisa Beddell, Lucy Jane Bledsoe, Sinead Norton Boland, Andrew Brimelow, Peter Bromley (2 stories), Anne Brooke, Rebecca Bryant, Zoe Marie Bullingham, Kathryn Burke, Jo Campbell, Jo Cannon (2 stories), Bianca Cawthorn, Fleur Chapman, Andrew Clancy, Helena Close, Caroline Clough, Annis Cohen, Traci Oberg Connor, Helen Cowan, Judy Crozier (2 stories), Paula Cunningham, Ronald Currie, Jr., Stephen Cusack (2 stories), Lauren Elise Daniels, Carys Davies, Paul Bassett Davies, Lynn Dolman, Michael Donnellan, Jennifer A. Donnelly, Bryony Doran, Bruce Durie, Geona Edwards, Owen Egerton, Ann Eisenberg, Anthony Etherington, Eric Flamm, Sarah Flygare, Solveig Fos, Alex Fox, Clare Framrose, Megan Frazer, Sean Gallagher, Lyn Gambles, Andrew Garvey, James Gerrard, Sonya Gildea, Owen Goodwyne, Pippa Gough, Rebecca Graham, Gordon Grant, M.S. Greenberg, Debra Grubb, Louis Gruber, John Hall (2 stories), Lewis Russell Hall, Gergely Hamar, Samuel E. Hamn, Tom Harper, Noel Harrington, Ruth M. Harris, Shane Harrison, Thomas J. Harrison, Antonia Hart (2 stories), Justina Hart, Paul Harvey, Eli Hastings, Jonathan Haylett, Tim Hayton, Patricia Heane, Bonnie Hearn Hill, Matthew Hilbert, Hanh Hoang, Thomas Hocknell, Susan Holland, J.B. Hollander, Annie Holmes, Aileen Izett, Vanessa Jackson, Kunthavai Jayadevan, Phil Jell, Rosemary Jenkinson, Rita Jerome, David Jonas, Roger Jones, Meena Kaur, Hugo Kelly, Roy Kesey, Diana Keyes, Juergen Kinghorst, Gerard Kinsella, Annie Kirby, Helen Kitson, Susi

Klare (2 stories), Troy Klith, Susan Knight, Caroline Koeppel, Conor Laffan, Dyland Landis, Pamela Lane, Joshua Leavitt, Tom Lee, Mary Leland, Mick Looby, Sean Lusk, Ian J. MacLeod, Mo McAuley, Dunya McCammon, Maxwell McCann, Bonnie McCune, Patrick McCusker (2 stories), Sean McFadden, Tony McGettigan, Nell McGrath, Andrew McGuinness, Kath McKay, Ian Madden, Joshua Malbin, Linda Mannheim, Chris Marshall, Brendan Mathews, Karen Meredith, James Musgrave, Manini Nayar, Tomás O'Beirne, Gayle O'Brien, Stephen O'Connell, Garret O'Malley, Marcella O'Malley, Paddy O'Reilly, Elizabeth Oness, David Oprava, Nan Peacocke, Sylvia G. Pearson, Sue Peet, Susan Petrone, Marc Phillips, Jane Pidcock, Hilary Plews, Ron Praymak, Richelle Putnam, Gary Quinn, Sarah Quigley, David Rea, Glynis Reed, Joanne Riccioni, Robyn Rose, Mary Catherine Ross, Joyce Russell (2 stories), Astrid E. Sauge, Jane Seaford (2 stories), Ian Seed, Jane Sellers, Justin Smallpiece (2 stories), David E. Smith, Geoff Smith, Susie Stead, Lynn M. Stegner, M.M. Stockman, Kevin G. Summers, Penelope Kahler Swan, Marianne Taylor, James Terry, Caregan Thomas, Rhys Timson, Gerald Toth, Kate Tough, Trevor Trotman, Barry Troy (5 stories), Angela Uttley, Shubha Venugopal, David Veronese, Alan Walsh (2 stories), Sarah Wedderburn, John Welch (2 stories), John Wheway, Tobias Williams, Beth Williamson, Laura Williamson, Sheila Windsor (2 stories), Ellen Wise, Michael Winter, Muriel Winter, Keith Wright, James Young.